FAR

QUIET
FLOWS
THE
Una

Translated from
the Bosnian by Will Firth

istrosbooks

First published in 2016 by
Istros Books
London, United Kingdom www.istrosbooks.com

Originally published in Bosnian as *Knjiga o Uni*, by Buybook, Sarajevo

© Faruk Šehić, 2016

The right of Faruk Šehić to be identified as the author of this work has been
asserted in accordance with the Copyright, Designs and Patents Act, 1988

Translation © Will Firth, 2016

Illustrations and cover art: Aleksandra Nina Knežević
Typesetting and design: Davor Pukljak, www.frontispis.hr

ISBN: 978-1-908236-49-4

Printed in England by
CPI Group (UK) Ltd, Croydon, CR0 4YY

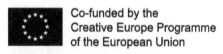

Co-funded by the
Creative Europe Programme
of the European Union

The European Commission support for the production of this publication does not constitute an
endorsement of the contents which reflects the views only of the authors, and the Commission
cannot be held responsible for any use which may be made of the information contained therein.

Supported using public funding by
**ARTS COUNCIL
ENGLAND**

LOTTERY FUNDED

Contents

Forgetting is a form of memory, its vague basement, the other, secret, side of the coin.

JORGE LUIS BORGES

My mind forgets, but my body keeps the score.
The body is bleeding history.

GEOFFREY HARTMAN

Hypnosis

One

Sometimes I'm not me, I'm Gargano. He, that other, is the real me: the one from the shadow, the one from the water. Blue, frail and helpless. Don't ask me who I am because that scares me. Ask me something else. I can tell you about my memory: about the world of solid matter steadily evaporating and memory becoming the last foundation of my personality, which had almost completely vaporized into a column of steam. When I jump into the past, I'm fully aware of what I'm doing. I want to be whole like most people on this Earth. Now I feel better, staring at the unbroken white line on the steel-blue asphalt. It soothes me. Darkness falls painlessly. I don't look back. The dark is behind me, but it feels like it's not there at all; not swallowing up the road, the buildings and the trees. It walks along behind me but dares not come close because it knows that then I would have to use my shield of paper with luminous words, and everything would go down the drain. And no one wants that to happen: neither Gargano, nor the dark, nor that other, meaning me – the astronaut, the adventurer and explorer of rivers and seas.

My memories are ugly and dirty. I feel disgust when I have to talk about the way things were in Yugoslavia and the start of the war. Poor boys in the piss-stinking changing room before PE lessons. The very sight of the school building made me break into a cold sweat under my jumper, which was so tight that I got attacks of claustrophobia. How could I forget? We found salvation from the school's excessive military discipline in the toilet block, where the concentration of ammonia took your breath away. The teachers were strict and starched, the corridors polished like rifle barrels, and the blackboard was black with grey stripes from the sponge with chalky water. Cigarette butts and condoms floated in the toilet bowls: the only form of rebellion against the crusty establishment. All of us had to wear identical blue dustcoats. The air in the corridors smelt of school sandwiches made with the cheapest salami (pompously named 'Parisian'). Given its architecture, the school could immediately be turned into a barracks in the event of war because it had a mass of small windows, from which we, little soldiers, our faces defiant and sooty, with slingshots and stone-firing wooden guns, would offer resistance to the numerically superior, insidious enemy, while singing Partisan songs during lulls in the fighting.

The rotten floorboards in the tenements dating back to Austro-Hungarian times stank of stale faeces and the diseases of their tenants; the lumpenproletariat of my home town, Bosanska Krupa. The neck of the pint bottle of beer peered out of the forest around Striborova's mature vagina when the waitress showed customers what her organ could do. She lay on the table with her big snow-white thighs spread wide and her ponytail of satiny black hair hanging down at the back of her head, and a vein as thick as a finger bulged on her neck. The light on the high ceiling flickered, and those with poor sight came up close to convince themselves of this voracious vulva. When she had finished her performance, she collected money, pulled on her long white drawers, let down her short skirt and went back to pouring brandy for the thirsty spectators. If those bystanders, sodden with cheap brandy and reeking of nicotine, read Latin books, they would know they'd just had the good fortune of peering into the *speculum mundi*, the mirror of the world.

The memories are so ugly that they neutralize themselves. Everything I remember makes me stop rewinding the story. I see horse droppings steaming on the asphalt of Tito Street. I hear the clatter of horses' hooves – a relentless, depressive beat that unnerves me. The rain falls for days in the rhythm of the horseshoes. I know I can suppress that feeling of nausea and see everything in more beautiful colours, but then I feel I'll betray my wish for an uncompromising view of the past.

A coffin with a glass window emerges from my memory: my art teacher is scowling at me through it with his black-rimmed glasses, and it's as if that black frame has already downsized his face to the format of an obituary notice, decades before he would be killed. I remember never-ending Partisan funerals, the trumpets and trombones of the brass band sounding their mournful notes, and sweat trickling down my spine from the marches I watched at nine-thirty on Sunday mornings on channel two of the State television. I see the open coffin with my great-aunt's body in a white bundle being lowered into the side of Hum Hill, from where you can look out over the green islands of the river. It was the lie we lived and which would come back at us through thousands of shells fired over the four years of the war. My disgust could take the form of a religion, but I don't want to give in to hatred. That would be too cheap and easy for my taste.

Too hot in the sun; cold and damp in the shade and the stench of urine, excrement and shoe polish. Those are the memories of my past life that first come to my senses. I don't think I'll ever be able to get over my disgust for the empty phrases the former State rested on. The very mention of those words makes me feel unwell. Luckily, we still have indirect speech and words with hidden meanings. And we have the River Una.

Two

Journalistic polymaths, those experts on everything, say it was a case of *force majeure*: a tectonic disturbance of history, a white hole in the nebulae of Asterion and a sub-spatial fluctuation within black matter, the collapse of the last utopia of the twentieth century, blah blah blah. The Berlin Wall came crashing down on us, so it was only fair that blood be let somewhere. Except that I wasn't a tiny cog in the workings of some cosmic powers – as a real man with a formed personality, I had one private mission: physical survival. Why should I believe those who have never smelt the odour of gunpowder on their own skin, which no detergent can wash off, when they don't believe me? If I needed anything, I did it myself. I took my fate into my own hands and didn't wait for a knock on the door in the wee hours and to be taken away and shot in a ditch. People always pay for passivity with their lives, and I had some living to do. Just then, I didn't think of my landlady from Zagreb, a giant old peasant woman, who said to me and my room-mate in 1990: 'The Serbs are gonna slaughter you all in Bosnia'. What could we have known back then, we tender-handed navvies enamoured of film and literature?

Post-scriptal analysts have trouble understanding the struggle for survival because they like to bandy around convoluted metaphors and explain my fate with global processes and events of crucial significance, pseudo-events that will never be able to explain the cataclysm. The river of blood and the ruthlessness, the squeak of the tracks of a T-55 tank that makes your blood freeze even two kilometres away. I'm not going to list you all the fascinating images of horror I witnessed because that would take a book twice as thick as this, and the effect would be the same: whoever doesn't understand can simply remain in the blissful dark of ignorance.

My biography is a string of coincidences, many of my own choosing, but some of which chose me. If I was able to explain everything to myself, I might as well dig a grave and go and lie in it because there would be no point in living. My biography is about flesh and blood, not entertainment. I am somewhere there in the middle of it all. I am one, but there are thousands of us – the unbreakable broken ones.

I have to tell you this: I've killed a man, and not just one but several. When you're firing, all your worries vanish. Not every bullet finds its mark, of course, but some certainly do. When you're shooting, you're as light as a feather, and that pleasure could make you lift off the ground and hover for a moment, but you're in cover, lying belly-down in the churned-up soil, flattened grass and wet leaves, because that's what your instinct tells you to do. When I shoot, I feel like Jesus Antichrist. I deliver the very opposite of compassion. There are no pangs of conscience, and no one is going to whisper in your ear that the enemy is human too. Things are different on the battlefield: the enemy is the enemy. He cannot be human. The enemy has to be a slimy hymenopteran with horns and pig's trotters, so just fire away and don't worry about the nonsense that cowards and philosophers waste their time on. I killed several individual enemies in hand-to-hand combat, so now my fellow townspeople avoid me, and when I walk down the street everyone crosses to the other side. I can just smell their fear. It reeks of loathing, of Hegel and Kant, of the universal sense of human life and of so-called human kindness; all of which deserve my complete contempt.

I killed three men, and also an Autonomist from the 'Republic of Western Bosnia'. Killing is like a drug that knocks you off your feet and then suddenly lifts you up with the thrust of a rocket. When it lifts you like that you think you're on top of the world. I turned living bodies into apparitions like moths in the night. I am a poet and a warrior, and secretly a Sufi monk in my soul. A holy man, according to Baudelaire. I killed on battlefields those with forgotten and insignificant names, in all climatic conditions: when wet snow is falling, blood is red like in the film *Doctor Zhivago*, and one drop of blood and a little snow are enough to be able to draw a daisy with your finger.

Sometimes I asked myself why? What is the sense of killing? Now I know the answer, and I couldn't care less. I don't have any pangs of conscience because of the men I now imagine as ghostly portraits on photographs, where the heads have been cut out with scissors. Before long, they will depart my memory for the darkness. I never saw Pope Wojtyła anywhere in the combat zone, although the lichen on the trees resembled the colour of the spots on the back of his hands. In war, everything is so simple and clear. Except when blood gets under your fingernails – it's hard to wash off when it sets, and then you can't get it off for days.

I killed because I wanted to survive the chaos. I didn't know how else to do it, and my pride didn't allow me to spend the war in the units at the rear. There are those who did it differently to me: those who prayed to God that they might get hit, that they might be killed because they were full of life and strength, and that was what oppressed them – the fear they would stay alive with so much terrible energy in them. They didn't know what to do with it. That's what made them charge with eyes open and a pure heart, unafraid of where they were going. They had to charge because such was the life in them: stupendous and greater than death. But I was calm and knew what I was doing. I never got drunk or stoned at the front line I was always focused. That's why I'm able to tell you this now. Dead mouths don't talk, as you know. I'm not unfeeling, in case you think that, just honest. I'm a bit like a Nazi: I like to listen to Bach played with a Stihl chainsaw. Black & Decker isn't bad either.

Three

The forests were turquoise and the trees swayed gently from side to side like the arms of a sea anemone. That was the scene in the distance, on the edge of the horizon, as seen through the fogged-up windowpane, a rainbow filter, because I was exercising my imagination. The trees were actually bare and ash grey, covered with lichen and the occasional ball of mistletoe, whose green had no connection at all with the general dearth of chlorophyll in nature and in people's souls. Colours were infiltrated agents of the Western world; they smacked of luxury and opulence and as such had to be banished from our lives. On this side of the windowpane I was the lord of indoor reality. Outside in the streets, other stories applied. Beneath my balcony lay a town that I still couldn't feel was my own – I was too young for that kind of love – a soft town like warm vomit in the sun. For me back then, the State was like a distant sphere from the *Atlas of Celestial Bodies*. Later I became very fond of it, despite the supernatural effort being made to conceal all the differences between us with the tall tale of us all being brothers and sisters, and about everything in Yugoslavia being the best, while misery, squalor and debauchery flourished in both the East and the West. What a twangy word: debauchery. I felt like a stranger in my own town when I realized we weren't all brothers and sisters – not because I didn't want us to be – but because there was no good will among most of the local Serbs and Croats. Not to mention the ridiculous situation when I did my compulsory military service in the 'Yugoslav People's Army' and had to state my ethnicity: since I came from a Bosniak family, the Serbs and Croats tried to persuade me to write 'Bosnian Muslim' because Yugoslavs didn't really exist, they said. Yes, I lived an identity that was marginal in the very country named after it. The biggest shock for me was when I discovered that the number of people who identified themselves as Yugoslavs was statistically tiny. When I finished school and went off to do my military service, my mother advised me to declare myself a Yugoslav because she thought the other recruits would laugh at me if I said I was a Muslim. Both her suggestion and that of my comrades were beside the point because I was enamoured of the Spanish Civil War. I regretted not being able to return by time machine to Spain and die fighting for freedom. Only there, in that short period, did *my* nation exist.

'Who leads our struggle?' yelled the tired voice beneath my balcony that was heading a column of young people on their way back from a communal work project. Like when a diver brings up a dead body from the raging river on a length of cable, so the foremost voice pulled along all the others.

'Tiii-to!' reverberated from a hundred throats.

'What are we part of?'

'The Peeeo-ple!'

'What guides and bonds us?'

'The Paaar-ty!'

I recognized the faces in the first few rows. They had the look of automatons and were drooling for a big serve of army-style bean stew from the field kitchen. That was what the lofty ideal of *ongoing revolution* boiled down to, it seemed. The voice ascended through the centre of town towards the hospital, to be drowned out by car horns and the yelling of public drunkards. A guy called Yup stood out among these: a paunchy, lumbering man who resembled a bun, and when he had no firewater he was like a greasy, ill-tempered rodent. Not so his father, Yup Senior, with his tiny, bird-like physique, gold signet ring and hair always slicked back the old-fashioned way with brilliantine: he pickled himself calmly and with class, as befits a baron of the bottle. The guy from the League of Young Communists shouting his questions, whose answers were as irrefutable as the existence of a second horn on a unicorn, had an indigo tear tattooed on his cheek – the 'medal' of the infamous Zenica House of Correction.

Somewhere in this catalogue of disgust and attraction was the nasal sing-song of the blind Romany who used to stand with his creased face and matted black hair in the town marketplace every Monday of the late 1980s, amidst the masses that stank of sweat and fresh curd cheese.

'Give me alms, good ladies, comrades, young folk...
A small donation, may God giii-ve yoo-u heee-alth...
May God proteee-ct your children...'

This people's Homer stood like a statue at the side of the street chanting his prayer, which reconciled communism and Islam. Early in the mornings, his family would take him there to beg and leave him to do his work. When the market was over, they would come and take him away again like a Sony robot with rusty works. Sometime before the war, Homer left for the south with the swallows. I could have sworn that for four years after that no one saw a single swallow.

I couldn't help feeling I was in the grips of a perverse fascination by being attracted to what disgusted me at the same time. It's like when you look down from a balcony: you're drawn to that drop, but you don't take a casual step into thin air like the suicide jumper whose goal is the car park below. You've probably thought about your stomach while holding a long kitchen knife in your hand – well, it's the same perverse fascination that takes hold of me whenever I think about life in former Yugoslavia and its break-up.

Four

You don't get dizzy from watching the river flow. If you start talking about something you'll soon lose the thread because the water takes hold of you and you forget the words you wanted to say, and *Enjoy the Silence* by Depeche Mode plays in your ears. We enjoyed watching the Una as it flowed now fast, now sluggishly, and its restless surface spread peace all about.

We avoided our brigade's anniversary event because we had no time for stuffy observances in the mood of the old system, which still hung over us like an undead spirit. The factory buildings on the outskirts of town were like that too, where people had already begun salvaging usable sheet metal. The carcasses of factories and Serbian houses were to be thoroughly pillaged and dismantled, down to the last brick. Who now remembers all those bizarre deaths of wretches who were crushed by the concrete ceilings of abandoned houses where they'd been chiselling bricks out of the walls? Beginning in September 1995, and continuing for some months, caravans of tractors, trucks and horse-drawn carts passed through the town loaded with plunder from villages in the Grmeč mountain range, heading for places some way away. The lust for other peoples' property is a strange and widespread malaise.

We got together on our brigade's anniversary to celebrate a lot of things we didn't want to call by their names. We toasted in a cheerful Zen manner, without clicking bottles and without excessive exclamations. Our alcohol-fuelled jaunt of favourite locations inevitably took us to a caravan selling drinks in the shade of Japanese plum trees. Our legs led us there all by themselves. The shade was perfect, the booze too, and our stories left reality far behind. Later, someone suggested we go and see the freshly renovated hall of the Culture Centre because we all loved buildings untouched by fire – they were a direct physical link to our past. We could take a peek behind the heavy brocade curtains, where cinematic illusions were shown. King Kong's sadness because of his impossible love for a woman was palpable there in the damp air, accompanied by sighs and tears. My best memory from that hall was the visit of a troupe of Italian magicians sometime in the late 1970s. They charmed cobras and skewered a midget woman with swords in a wooden cube, only for her to hop out again cheerful and unharmed, in a bathing suit, to the general enthusiasm of the gullible audience; and they performed many lesser and greater miracles, too. There were the fakir's mass hypnoses, where a boy would climb up a rope suspended in the air, or the fakir would chop up the boy with a machete and put his parts in a basket, only to bring him out in one piece afterwards.

The Ramayana Flying Circus from India was to perform that evening. The hypnotist was having a dress rehearsal and needed a guinea pig. And suddenly there was me: an aspiring poet and veteran of our dear war. Why the fakir chose me of the three of us remains a mystery to me. I had only just made myself comfortable, leaning back in the leather-upholstered chair in the middle of the Culture Centre's empty hall. Apart from the scar cutting diagonally across my face, there was nothing else that made me stand out.

Before the war, the hall could take an audience of seven hundred on fold-up seats, and when King Kong, Godzilla or Bruce Lee were screened people would sit on the floor, too. I didn't get to see the main entrance or the stage with the heavy brocade curtains. The sun and the birdsong in the poplars and the luxuriant black walnut trees remained outside. My two friends had played a trick on me by bringing me here, under the pretext of showing me the renovated hall. They had actually hoped to see circus animals, especially drunken dancing monkeys.

'Not too long ago, I think sometime after the war, a circus came to the football stadium in Banja Luka. A guy who went to see it told me there was a magician with a young monkey on a chain – a mandrill or baboon, he couldn't say exactly – and the magician started to swing the chain. The monkey lifted off the ground and flew around in circles above the magician's head in front of five thousand people. And do you know what it did?'

'No, what?' I asked the guy.

'It held on to the chain as tightly as it could, like a little person,' he tittered with a smoker's laugh.

My friends and I went in the side door, holding our bottles of beer, and ran into a fakir with a torch in his hand. It was rather disquieting to see a bearded man in a long robe standing and staring at us. He seemed to have been expecting us because he wasn't surprised at us being there. We struck up a polite conversation about the authenticity of mass hypnosis, after which the fakir pointed his finger at me, switched off the torch and vanished into the pitch darkness. My heart started to beat like a drum. I've always been one for unusual challenges – the crazier the better.

The light fled at familiar speed through the narrow gap between the doors as my company vanished. When I found a chair and slumped into it, a spotlight went on up on the stage. I pushed my bottle of beer under my chair. The temporal bond between my pre-war and post-war life had been broken, and the discontinuity had to be bridged. Because I want to be whole again, if only in memory, I would have to become a time traveller and go back to the past: that would mean attempting the impossible task of over-flying the war and overcoming my own queasiness in order to find that temporal bond to join the past and the present. It seemed to be the first time in my life that there was an advantage in having a scar on my face. If it attracted demented, neurotic women and half-mad men, was I one of them too, marked with a shadow of disfigurement – a freakish, dark aureole above my head? The answer was affirmative. This kind of magnetism isn't exactly a blessing. But the scar became my ticket to the show.

Five

The hypnotist strode on to the stage in a turban with chilled-out, hissing little snakes, and in that instant a mist rose to my knees. Behind his back, a wind broke everything before it, blowing over barren wastes from the stacked loudspeakers. And I thought I heard the electric bellow of little plush elephants, which I remembered having heard in the streets of Sarajevo, where freeloaders sold them to bustling crowds. Our time has vanished, I thought for a moment as my gaze dropped from the ceiling of the hall to the wall above the stage, where letters had been scratched out of the slogans extolling Tito, the people and the Party, and proclaiming eternal life for all. Since I didn't have a single pre-war photograph, how else could I think about my past other than as something non-existent. I closed my eyes and ran the excellent black and white video spot of *Wonderful Life* for myself on the inside of my eyelids. And I'll attach that video as a last piece of evidence that my intimate world from the past did exist, even though I myself sometimes thought I'd invented my memories. The sounds of the wind slowly receded, muffled by the crackling of a record that hypnotically repeated one and the same sound. I was at some kind of fanciful investigation.

No need to run and hide
It's a wonderful, wonderful life...

Each time the hypnotist spoke a number; I would arrange tsunamis of thoughts into meaningful wholes and turn them into confessional statements. I already had faithful listeners, whom I could tell anything to for hours, but this was a different experience. Now I was like a switch on a device for decoding people's lives and just needed to be flicked. I was an optical instrument – an eyepiece, lens tube and magnifying glass – crossed with a long-necked orchid, and I would blazon forth stories through its trumpet.

The choice of music was unusual because normally a relaxing soundtrack is used to induce hypnosis. The white-bearded fakir stood in the bright circle of the spotlight on the stage, as straight as a candle. His eyes were grey and cold, his mien as clear as mud. When he had finished the countdown induction, he told me in broken Bosnian:

'Now you returning to your own past, your childhood... Your head is clear and cold. How old are you?'

'Thirteen,' I told him.

'You are sure?'

'Yes, I'm thirteen and I've just left the house to go fishing. I'm wearing gumboots, and I have a fishing rod and an angler's rucksack. The bullrushes smell of fish mucus. There are so many fish that you never tire of watching them. It's like the feeling of a miser fondling his gold – he can't get enough of it. I check the bubble float, which has to be half full of water, and I grease the artificial flies so they will stay on the surface. I cast all the way to the opposite bank and the bubble float lands on the soft, sandy shore covered with waterweed. It looks as if I've laid the float on a green pillow. Now I gently pull the line and the bubble float into the water because a prize trout is waiting just a metre or two downstream. It's a good 30 cm long, 24 cm being average. I have a hunch that this is going to be a long fight. I use the tip of the rod to unfurl the fishing line with the flies tied to it, and I give the last one a tweak so it goes right over the mouth of the big fish. I watch the fly breathlessly; the fish shoots up towards the surface, misses the fly and makes a big bubble in the water. The handhold of the rod is at my right hip and I immediately jerk it back like a gunslinger, and the float with the flies travels all the way back into the grass at my feet. It happened so quickly that I only saw the trout's white underside as its mouth snapped at the fly. I have to calm down, cast towards the green pillow again, and do everything from scratch once more. I'm so excited that I don't notice the people higher up on the bank kibitzing me and the fish...'

The artificial mist swallowed me at ant speed. I fell through time as though through pliant peat. As I sank through sparkling blackness and the pink light of silt, I caught a glimpse of houses growing out of the ground beneath my feet, and then spirals snaked up from their chimneys – a signal that life would put down roots by the River Una. The trees in the town's park were slim at the waist, and the town itself was brand new. I don't know who grew closer to whom, I to the town or it to me, but wherever I looked the town was there, within my grasp. I could change the years and decades, as I liked. I saw Grandmother Emina's house and knew I had to stop. The journey begins here and will be rounded off here, too, because this journey never ends. The mist enveloped me from feet to neck, stopping at the height of my polo neck. I'll tell everything – even what the fakir doesn't ask me.

Mariners of the
Green Army

There was a flash in the air, a festive explosion, and the circus of nature would announce pollen in the flowers and the triumph of green in the town's park. An incurable spring mood took possession of every thought and every tuft of grass, upsetting the schedules of airborne insects, which collided in the aerial avenues. There was drunkenness in the earth and the air that announced the birth of something splendid. Spring is that miracle that materializes like fireworks in the sky, when the shapeliness of every girl and woman is hormonally magnetic and that little Krakatoa in your trousers is primed to erupt.

I would pinch myself to make sure of my own mortality because we're made in the image of God, and for a moment I thought I was becoming ethereal with bliss.

Spring was that carnival that would bring the whole world to the brink of travesty. In the blink of an eye, a grey winter wasteland would become green Atlantic grass that we could sail through if only we were able to shrink to the size of an ant or a merry grasshopper. And that was very hard in a world ruled by adults, who tried to make us be like them in every way possible – frowning, moustachioed men who performed important tasks for the existence of our great and powerful State. But I didn't want a moustache and wasn't in a hurry to grow up.

I believed in the red of my Pioneer scarf. And in the blood of all earthly proletarians, who would close ranks in their dim, underground factories, thirsting for world revolution, when Marx, Engels and Lenin would raise them from the dead. Later it would just take Karlo Štajner's anti-Gulag classic *7000 Days in Siberia* for me to strike communism from the list of beloved, sacred 'isms' in my high-school diary, albeit it in pencil and with a wavering hand.

In the language of the Party, I had had become a revisionist; I was like Rosa Luxemburg, whom we hated because she had abandoned the true current of the revolution and become a vile agent of imperialism – at least that's the way it was served to us in the Marxist textbooks.

Everything had to be in the service of our powerful State, the fourth-largest military force in the world, whose wings of steel we were more than proud of. Even our town's park boasted small patriotic trees (more like bushes) planted with geometrical precision to form a socialist star in leaf. This large, foliate star was home to the nests of robin redbreasts, that working class contingent among the birds – a Red Army of uniform appearance that was far from possessing any talent in song but composed an industrious and obedient youth wing that forever wove its grey, hanging houses in those bushy trees, whose berries had a reddish juice with a bitter taste.

Still, robins were sweet-feathered creatures that always chirped and worked tirelessly to further their small, socio-political communities, creating a secure avian commune that functioned according to the principle *from each according to their abilities, to each according to their needs*. That really was a classless society because all its members had equal rights like in the hyperborean land of Sweden.

'Just you try walking on the grass!' Kosta the park warden would roar in his grey-green uniform and huge Russian fur hat, whose circle of shade could shelter a family with ten or more children.

'Even the grass will be red if the Central Committee so decides,' Kosta tried to scare us, invoking the grand masonic lodge that ran our great and powerful State – and all just because we loved to walk on the grass and pick the daisies and star-shaped dandelions. I was more afraid of his fur hat than his bony features, his face with broad cheekbones and ill-tempered, grey gimlet eyes that sent a glare instead of a greeting when he was officially cross. The total power of the State could be seen in the fact that even its lowest echelon, Kosta the park warden, was perfectly intimidating.

We avoided him like the plague, and we would wait for him to go down the road into town reciting the Party slogans he had learned by heart, which could even make the bark of the robinias seem smooth and soft. Then we would dash to the wild and irre-pressible bushes with sturdy rods sprouting yellow petals all along their length; we called them *magelana*, but later I discovered they were forsythia. These were our boats, which we named after the famous Portuguese seafarer Ferdinand Magellan.

Every *magelana* could fit two sailors and a captain. Our *magelanas* grew close together, so we could see and call to each other on our imaginary journeys. It was best when a warm spring breeze came up, and then it was like a gale that strained at the ropes of our ships and rocked us on the branches like mariners fighting against a raging sea. Everything started to spin around us – the grass, the trees, the gravel on the paths and the houses nearby. That was the moment when we were freed of gravity. The Earth turned and the world hung above us, but we gave resolute orders and bravely put out into the wide sea of the sky. We sailed without fear, with our hearts as astrolabe and compass.

Look, this is where that marvellous tree used to be, whose trunk was completely covered in ivy, so it was easy to climb up its tough veins into the crown, where you really couldn't tell which leaves were the tree's and which belonged to the velvety creeper. I would climb up into that crown, to where it was quiet and peaceful inside. The darkness there was my ally, while the main thoroughfare of Marshal Tito Street ran below it, full of comings and goings: people, cars, horse-drawn carts, ambulances, stooped peasant women... But there were also upright ones carrying heavy loads on their heads; women whose necks were surely able to carry whole slabs of the world, chunks their households rested on. Old men passed by too, bitterly spitting out something akin to the acrimony of their lives. Everything was in motion: lines of lizards, ants and red-black beetles, columns of cattle, sheep from the high pastures of the Grmeč range, nomadic shepherds in fur hats like those of Cossacks, the blind and the drunk, children and youth, workers who were also drunkards, and torrents of people who knew nothing and expected nothing, because no one could see the future. It was guaranteed by the weight of the big stone letters up on Tećija Hill that spelled the name of the greatest son of all the Yugoslav peoples.

Up in the tree, in the peace and quiet, I was perfectly invisible. I didn't exist. I could even close my eyes and the world would become insignificant. I would be all by myself, a small light in the darkness, before the storm blowing in from Grmeč. One body, nothing more, that shivered with cold as the wind rushed through the green branches. From my vantage point I watched ordinary life, the secret life beneath the town's park, by the side of the asphalt road that Kosta went down into the history of the night, marshalling clouds and elusory celestial bodies. Apart from the enticing female hips, the sea was peaceful, with no waves and agitation. Past and future was all the same. O people, flow like you are water! I was terribly afraid of death, but wherever I looked it was not to be seen.

Watching the
Fish

I am an Earth-bound astronaut, and I travel without movement and goal. The atmosphere is my prison. If only I could roam the vacuum of outer space, albeit shut away in a wooden rocket with a porthole, I would perhaps say: 'Planet Earth is blue and there's nothing I can do.' What sweet dreams! I am an Earth-bound astronaut, and I travel at the speed of thought. I won't live to see the picturesque vision of battle cruisers in flames at the edge of the constellation Orion – the film will have to do. Nor will I see the blond replicant played by Rutger Hauer in Blade Runner *sitting at the top of a building, completely naked and with his legs crossed, saying his famous: 'Time to die', before closing his eyes and expiring in the incessant rain from the dark sky. I won't break through the stratosphere, behind which no one knows where fiction ends and reality begins, and vice versa. All the SF films are happening up there in the universe right now.*

I have butterflies because it will soon be dawn.

I make a pair of binoculars with my hands and watch the Evening Star, the last to leave its watch post. Summer is no time to die, some elderly people said yesterday as they gazed at the main current of the river from the wooden bridge. But the stars go out like souls leaving bodies – suddenly and quickly – I once read in a paperback with a dubious title. My reality is boring and a long way from fantasy; and, I don't like realistic books.

Instead, I muse that my heart beats in time with distant galaxies. For me, night isn't a time when ghosts from a mass of former lives come out and stop you from sleeping. Night for me is a vacuum, a gap between the setting and the rising of the sun; a necessary evil. I wait for daybreak so as to slip out from under the heavy quilt in my grandmother's house – it can be chilly even in June – because I can't wait to slip on my Bermudas and espadrilles, climb the concrete stairs pot-holed by the rain, and come to the mossy abutment where orange-coloured slugs have left shiny trails of slime. I want to travel those rainbow highways with the pad of my finger and follow them all the way into the holes and cracks until my finger can go no further. That inability to enter small worlds, to creep inside the stem of a plantago leaf or the tightly closed bud of a white rose, would hound me in much more terrible times, too.

The walls of my grandmother's house are thick and warm because tufa stone from the riverbed has been built into them. A clock hangs on the wall above my head and its hand ticks haltingly across the unintelligible inscription Tempus Vulnera Curabit, and whenever I read those words I shrink like a boiled shirt.

The slugs' slimy bodies sometimes look darker: they're red and brown in the cold lee cast by the long, three-storey buildings nearby; later they become a transparent yellow in the rays of the sun. It rises above the dew-wet tiles of the tallest house in the neighbourhood, which looks to me like a medieval castle that no one can come out of happy. The eyes of a boy follow me pleadingly from its windows. He's my age but afflicted by premature ageing. The lines of his face show a haggard old man with the eyes of an innocent boy. He waves to me and smiles from a window that frames him like an icon.

The spindly waifs without so much as a house on their backs emerge from cracks in to which fine fingers of moss grow. Their antennae timidly probe the morning air. Cold scalpels. When I touch them, they quickly retract and the slugs stop furrowing their sticky trenches. The sun will turn them into little roads in all the colours of the rainbow, spectral Golgothas, on which no one will be crucified.

The softness of their bodies was shocking and stirring, so I loved and pitied them at the same time. I didn't understand how a tender body could become a dry, lifeless remnant in the midday sun. Afterwards I would reluctantly realize that they, too, had their end like every other living thing.

I got up and ran to see the slugs every morning until a mysterious crime happened. Some pedant had peeled the moss from the retaining wall and covered up the cracks with mortar. Without a doubt, that killer of nature was an over-ambitious person, surly and morbidly industrious. Who was he? An old man who wanted to iron out every irregularity on the surface of the Earth? A carpenter obsessed with geometry, hated any gnarls and knobs in his wood – excrescences reminiscent of frozen stellar spirals? A mason with a bitter trowel in his heart horrified at the emptiness around us and condemned to furiously build and build? Who was that malefactor who strove to kill imagination?

I mourned for the slugs for two days and soon forgot about them. I had to shrug off that bittersweet mourning and find something new. It was then that I discovered fish. They're free and cannot be walled in because water is a realm of freedom. Fish are large, elegant submarines with scales that cast gentle reflections through the water and the air. Pike, faster than arrows, bask in the sun on the surface between the threads of swaying bullrushes, from where they shoot out towards their prey. I discovered whiskered barbel – bottom feeders, which anglers used to feed leftovers of roast lamb. Then there are roach and sneep – the grazing cows of the river. I discovered grayling – *icthyo* torpedoes that launched out of the water to swallow fluorescent-green flies with gluttonous repetition. Trout, the unchallenged masters of the cascades and rocky riverbeds. Some people can tell the future by reading coffee grounds, but I learned to watch the fish.

Here at the beginning, it would make sense for me to go back to our origins: to the water we're made of and the swirling currents of the underwater epic, where I'll hearken to the anarchist trout and their fulsome chatter. You'll find out later why the trout are anarchist. 'Fulsome chatter' is Rimbaud, I'll be a hypnotized boat, and the rivers will carry me wherever I wish.

The
Water's Republic

The Una and its banks were my refuge – an impenetrable fastness of green. Here I hid from people beneath the branches in leaf, alone in the silence, surrounded by greenery. All I could hear was my own heartbeat, the flutter of a fly's wings and the splash when a fish threw itself out of the water and returned to it. It's not that I hated people, I just felt better among plants and wild animals. When I entered the covert of the river, nothing bad could happen to me any more.

One of the Una's branches, the Unadžik, flowed past my grandmother's slanting house that was slowly sinking into the deposits of sand and silt brought by the raging water in the forceful April floods. The riverbed was of tufa overgrown with waterweed. Mussels with mother-of-pearl mirrors stuck out of its fine yellow sand, and lively eels wriggled. Where the bed was covered with stone, we used to catch bullheads using forks tied with wire to dead branches, and we would put our catch in large jars so we could watch them and marvel at their slippery bodies.

In places you could see a wood stove or a rusty washing machine, worn-out chestnut pans or old car parts at the bottom of a greenhole – our word for deep, green pools in the river. The water was so transparent and clear that a coin could be seen several metres down, reflecting the dial of the sun.

Each house had its own sewage system, whose contents would come thundering out into the river through a concrete pipe. When the water level dropped in the summertime, those cast-concrete maws of mortar welded to the ground resembled lazing crocodiles that would periodically belch out faeces and the froth of washing-machine detergent. Grayling, barbel and chub would gather in those places to feed on what people had been unable to digest.

Standing on those crocodile carcasses, anglers would cast sinkers and hooks with maggots, earthworms and bread. They used hand-crafted flies, coated with a special grease (to stop the feathered imitation from sinking) to lure and snag fine specimens of grayling, which they would pull up on to the bank together with the bubble float. The whopper would thrash about in a dense patch of stinging nettles, tangling up the thin line and all the other flies tied to the main line, which passed through the ceramic rings of the rod and ended in the shiny spool of a Shakespeare or D·A·M Quick reel.

Brown trout with red and black dots hovered solemnly and motionlessly in front of a rock or just above a slab of tufa, usually closer to the far bank, and would loudly launch themselves out of the river to swallow mayflies that fell into the water in the gloaming. Their leaps made shivering circles that would gradually disperse on the peaceful surface like smoke rings in the fug of a bachelor's flat. With the coming of night, dragonflies would buzz above the Unadžik: blue-black males and greenish females – light river cavalry supported by a cacophony of owls, cuckoos and nightingales. The river sang a nocturne.

Autumn,

the Moss-grown Horseman from the North

Every year at the end of August a weed with pale-blue flowers ran riot in my Grandmother's courtyard that gently sloped down the sandy bank towards the river. I didn't know their name, but I called them blue loners. They would bashfully start to flower in June, but August was their promised month.

The calf becomes sirloin steak and schnitzel at the butcher's
The butcher has strong hands and ruddy cheeks
A charge through the grass with tin soldiers
Kinder Surprises produce Vikings of bronze.

Downstream, the blue loners were nourished by blood from the butcher's shop in a basement, whose drainpipe came out in the middle of the bank; from there, the blood seeped calmly towards the water.

The houses held their never-ending vigil looking down on the river bank, while stands of corn watched over the river's silence from the other side. People in their houses dreamed their civilian dreams about loans, working hours, football and fish. In the evenings, the ethereal fish would enter through the balcony doors and roam the whitewashed rooms, keeping watch over the Una's people, pausing above the anglers' foreheads and blessing them; those fish of air, clean and slender, with glittering tails, would enter people's thoughts. True anglers catch fish because they have no other way of showing them their wonderment. Some of them even kiss the fish before putting them back in the water. Dawn will break the spell and the sun will take possession of the balcony. Dawn emerges from the Una, borne by the mists and vapours of the river. The intangible fish expire, people awake, and thus the circle is constant every night.

The petals of those blue flowers were separate from each another like Omar Sharif's front teeth, so that they looked like propellers made of sky. Their colour was unreal amid the darkened, porous chlorophyll that reached its peak and then gently slid away towards the eddies of decay, before autumn tuned its instruments and struck up its symphony of dankness, rain and water vapour. It's hard not to love humidity – the soul of the soil, and what we're made of. I thought it impossible for such a shade of blue to exist in nature. I believed an invisible dyer went round at night and during the reign of the coppery mists and painted the flowers with diluted blue vitriol. A dragonfly with a human face; a harlequin of the earth with spikes of wheat in place of hair; a god of green and growing things, whom we would never see.

For me, plants were the world's greatest secret, a proud aristocracy of chlorophyll that didn't believe in life after death, and which, one day, when the hour came, would finally cover the whole world. They were a succulent essence, which you could only penetrate mechanically, leaving green juice all over your hands – the blood they didn't care about and gave so amply because they were eternal and indestructible in their spring awakenings.

As the glossy green of the other weeds faded, the cornflower intensified its azure. The late glory of the cornflower heralded the death of the summer by the Una – the coming of chill morning mists and shivering dusks, and the fickle sun would only warm faintly at its height because as soon as a wind blew from the water it spent no more warmth.

Then autumn would descend like a horde of Huns down the Točile and Kolajevac hills, beneath which flowed the River Krušnica – six kilometres long and as cold as the Bering Sea. The vegetation had no chance before such an onslaught. Autumn made cascades of watercolour leaves flow through the forests on Točile Hill, and their murmur was pure melancholy. Autumn would enter our chests through the ether we inhaled, to be distilled into the purest emotion, which tightened our throats and moistened our eyes with boyish sorrow. Then I would begin to read books about magic kingdoms in preparation for the winter, and after that I would wait

for the earth to cast off its snow so the yellow trumpets of primrose
could again announce the turmoil and pleasures of spring:

May I introduce myself: I am the King of Leaves
I am the opposite of the moss-grown horseman
The grain beneath the snow will sense me
Wild geese bear me on their wings.

Growing with the
Plants

A summer shower caught me behind the main grandstand of the FC Meteor stadium as I walked briskly along the gravel path to go swimming at Ajak, where an arm of the Una passed under a small bridge of creosoted railway sleepers to join the Krušnica. We used to swim in the greenhole in front of the bridge, while the central sleepers of the bridge were reserved for sunbathing. Further downstream the water was alive with chub and brown trout. Once I nearly drowned in that greenhole, and, strangely enough, that early brush with death only reinforced my love of the water.

Cumulonimbus clouds, swollen with moisture, drifted swiftly across the sky like in a speeded-up sequence of a documentary on the seething exuberance of the living world. I began to run as hot drops came down on me like big, mother's tears. My sodden white T-shirt clung to my body. I jumped seething puddles, enjoying the crazy feeling of freedom that filled my chest and spread through my veins. I was a land-dwelling dolphin, a flying squirrel, a fiery flamingo pacing across mudflats that smelt pure and pristine.

That feeling of freedom blurred my reason and intoxicated me with the raindrops, and I stopped at every flower whose pollen the rain had smudged, stroked the broad leaves of a plantago, ran my finger down a blade of wild barley and gazed at the molehills evaporating the earth's abundant warmth. What osmosis!

I thought I could fly with euphoria, like in a dream when I lift off in a sitting position, and simply wave my outstretched hands instead of wings and soon rise up above the ground. I float over the treetops and the roofs of familiar houses, always close to the ground, hoping for a soft landing the moment the enchantment wore off. Except that this now was a dream with my eyes open, a vision on a river island beneath a rainy sky. Not for a second could I see what was to come as I stared at the network of veins on a leaf, still green, that the wind had torn off; as I fingered the oily fin of a grayling; or as I kneaded a lump of red clay from Hum Hill in my hand. Like I say, there were no symbols and signposts towards what was to come. The war year 1992 was far away.

I came so close to meeting 'Smith the Redeemer', but he eluded me every time by hiding behind a screen of leaves, fleeing into the shade of a willow tree by the river, or jumping into the water and swimming to the other side. When he took the shape of a grass snake, cutting the water's surface in two like a giant zipper that threatened to spill open the whole world, swimming was in vain because he would already be on the opposite bank, striding with the pace of someone going home at dusk and leaving an aromatic trail of Solea sun cream and beer behind them. And I would quickly forget where my thoughts had gone off to and what kind of search I'd started out on, as I stood at the edge of the steep bank, while schools of little fish swam in the greenhole before my feet. They were bleak, which could never grow to more than 10 cm and so were good bait for going after voracious salmonids. Sometimes I felt sorry for catching them because they were so beautiful. Perfect and vulnerable. I would grab Smith the Redeemer by the lapel of his coat, he would have to stop, and I would pull him back so we were standing face to face at a respectable distance and I would ask him questions from the future:

Where would my books from the shelf above the Grundig TV set go?

What would happen to the television with the soft-touch command panel?

Where would my original cassettes disappear to, which were stacked above the books, a good hundred of them?

Where would all my letters go – love letters, as well as more trivial ones?

Where would my numismatic collection end up, including the gold florin with the countenance of Franz Josef and a copper coin from 1676 with the word *soldo* embossed on it, which was perforated because someone had worn it as a good-luck charm around their neck?

Where would my room go?

Why would there be nothing left in our flat but bare walls and gaping holes where the sockets and the toilet bowl used to be?

Who would steal all my photos, and on which of the countless heaps of rubbish would they shrivel in the sun like autumn leaves?

Who would read my copy of Zvonko Veljačić's novel about a space-travelling boy hero?

Who would take the Super 8 cinema projector and the tapes in the great cardboard boxes with film posters and credits on the lids?

Where would the black and white tape of *War of the Worlds* go?

Who would make all the things from our flat vanish 'just like that'?

Who would vacuum away our family history and make me think of the past as a gathering of amiable ghosts?

Would I be allowed to blame anyone, and whom would I accuse?

But, as I've said: 1992 was far away. There was no need for these questions from the near future because we were still in a holistic past, in the middle of the happy 1980s.

Dwarf corn grew in the sandy fields in the summers. Its sharp-edged leaves cut droplets of blood and the stalk would shake when it was showered with rain, which washed the sand from its knobbly roots. Tangles of tough veins sent minerals and water to nourish its living green. Armoured mole crickets dug their tunnels between the stalks, making the soil loose and porous. Anglers caught them and crammed them into fogged-up jars because they were a supreme delicacy for big chub.

The cloudburst ended abruptly, creating rainbow arcs in the rain-washed blue. The air had a savoury bitterness from the respiration of the plants. I watched them grow before my eyes. The first swathe of mowed grass smelt of lust: the aroma of orgasm and the vampire kiss of decay. And so I matured, hot and cold, together with the plants, and in my thoughts I wrote these lines:

The river is besieged by rain
An astonished mariner sinks beneath the tufa
The spirit of a mole-cricket whispers in his ear:
Melancholy is what defines us.

No Resurrection,
no Death

Contempt wasn't strong enough a word. The boy had done nothing to me, but I couldn't stand him. His appearance was irritating – perhaps he was good at heart, but you couldn't see it from the outside. That freak with the ungainly head too big for his body was one of the male scions of the Hodžić dynasty, which lived in the suburb of Žitarnica in a pedantically whitewashed house that radiated orderliness and a smell of modesty. Balloon-head Dino had a misshapen noggin like one of those plastic footballs you could buy for just a few coins at the Yugoplastika shop. That head was welded to a skinny torso with stalky little legs, and his arms were like insects' feelers. Flawed as he was, he didn't elicit any sympathy because of the malevolence you sometimes saw on his face. He didn't partake of any children's games and was quiet and withdrawn, probably because of the puritanical discipline instituted in their house by old Asim, the redeemer of pigeons, which he loved more than all other beings.

Grandfather Asim was the silver-haired head of the family who went out into the glazed-cement courtyard every morning with handfuls of breadcrumbs for the pigeons. He always called out *Vitiviti, vitiviti* to attract them, and the pigeons flew down devotedly like celestial dogs from the clean roofs to land on his head, shoulders and the arms he held out horizontally as if he was their Jesus. Soon he would be completely covered in them and the sun's light would refract on their neck feathers in a purple haze. When he walked, the pigeons didn't flee before him but balanced with their wings outspread to accord him their esteem. Their elated cooing filled the air of Žitarnica beneath the rocky slope of Hum Hill, that sacred mount of our childhood topography. A public toilet was built into the rock wall. It was a concrete bunker overgrown with ivy, a green-brown living thing with ivy veins and capillaries, where bubbles of ammonia welled from the earth and piles of faeces grew between the luscious green leaves. All this could mean only one thing: that drunks and lovers met here – those oblivious to the divine smells of human waste. Rows of prefab garages for the residents of nearby flats stood in front of the toilet, and next to them there rose an angular substation tower.

The old man's everyday bird-feeding helped him gather currency for the interstellar fuel he would need to reach heaven and be among the houris – the celestial beauties. He was so old that his skin resembled pure, fine cotton, in places transparent and pink. And his body, which looked like it was about to overcome gravity at any moment, was evocative of a time when people mixed with the cherubim, and it was as light as a feather from an angel's wing.

One morning I came out of Grandma Delva's house, sat on the steps and looked at the Mediterranean plants in flowerpots that she visited with ice-cold water at six o'clock every morning before the sun established its rule. The lemongrass gave off a strong scent, and beyond the concrete of the courtyard there grew long stalks similar to bamboo, which were hollow on the inside, but their green skin was strong and wouldn't break when you pressed it.

Through the wall of bamboo I saw Balloon-head moseying around the substation where there was a rusty barrel full to the brim with pondweed.

Drawn by curiosity, I ran up to him. The creep had thrown in several kittens, which were slowly drowning in the murky green water. I felt a pressure in my head like a black rod, and I punched him in his weedy stomach and drove him away. I pulled the kittens out and laid them on the grass. They looked so skinny with their fur plastered, wet and gleaming, having been licked by tongues of death. I moved them closer to the dense grass at the wall of the substation, hoping their mother would find them and revive them with her warm breath. But there was only earth beneath my feet as I stood dumbfounded above their little bodies, which lay there half-dead, with their eyes wide open.

I half-closed my eyes in despair and wanted to see old Asim, the redeemer of pigeons, revive the kittens, levitate to the top of Hum in rage and hurl bolts of lightning. He would howl old-Slavic prayers in a terrible voice and summon black crows from the clouds to punish all human evil. But that wouldn't be enough to return the kittens from the dead. Here, whoever dies is dead forever. Kittens go to heaven too, with their fur a-bristle.

Only old Asim refused to die, lying in his astronautically white room. In the hour of his death he became white as if covered by the first hoar frosts of winter. His pupils were snow-white heads of tailor's pins. He changed into a cotton jellyfish beneath the sheet and whisked out the window, loosening and tightening his cape-like body several times as jellyfish do. Only briefly did he hang in the air above the tumult of the streets before disappearing, escorted by a flock of white doves – far away from clay and worms, far away from cats and people.

Catching a
𝓕ish

'The Bulgie!'

That shout had an almost shamanic weight to it. 'The Bulgie' was an old woman who lived in a run-down Austro-Hungarian villa on the very bank of the Unadžik, where the river had made a particularly deep greenhole, and then flowed frothing through a narrow, stony channel beneath a wooden bridge and the old abattoir. The Bulgie lived alone in that big house, whose façade was crumbling due to the damp. There were orchards with long, swaying grass around her house, and we used to run through them, tearing bedewed cobwebs in our search for ripe apples. The old woman's nickname came from her late husband, who was allegedly Bulgarian, and the opaque greenhole just a few metres from her house was also known by that nickname.

'Bulgie's greenhole' was home to pike, chub, grayling, barbel, troutlet and adult trout. Willow branches on the opposite bank leaned over the water and lightly caressed the surface. Very large trout lurked there and would launch out at floating flies. The pikes were to be found closer to our bank, where they waited for the swarms of young fish. The bottom was sandy and silty from decayed leaves and wood. If you waded out into the silt, columns of air bubbles and the black ink of fossilized wood rose towards the surface. And everywhere there were calf's skulls, shoulder blades and other bones that the butchers dumped into the river from the wooden bridge. Inside the skulls that had almost become part of the tufa we used to find fat yellow maggots. They hid in cases made of sand and fragments of wood. First you take the maggot by the feelers on its brown head and pull it out of its case. When you take it out, it writhes like a new-born baby, and tries to wriggle out of your hand. We would put them in yoghurt containers or jars filled with water so they would stay fresh and alive. Then they were hooked, usually through the head, because if the maggot's body was punctured it oozed an ichor and puffed up like balloon. The yellow maggots were worth their weight in gold to anglers, and only passionate connoisseurs of the river knew where to find them. That maggot was the larva in the life cycle of an insect from the order of caddisflies (Lat. *Trichoptera*). We also called them 'water blossoms' or ephemeral mayflies because when they turned into winged adults after a year or two as larvae underwater, struggled free and made their hazardous way to the surface, they only lived for one more day.

Once my friend Sead and I caught an enormous pike near the Bulgie's. We cast and cast for hours, skilfully drawing metal lures through the water. It took Sead's spoon lure, and after a short fight he pulled a two-kilogram pike up onto the sandy bank, where I was hopping about with joy. How exciting is it when you see a fish open its white jaws and take the bait. The creature flashes in the water and turns its silver belly towards the surface. Afterwards it tries to get the lure out of its mouth by vigorously shaking its head from side to side, beautiful in its bewilderment. The rod bends from its weight like the letter omega. As I was trying to remove the three-headed hook from the pike's lower jaw, it bit me and bloodied the back of my hand. The pike's head was twice the size of my fist. Frightened and in pain, I hit it several times on the head, which was stupid because a pike's gill covers are sharp too. We returned home at dusk with the big fish, happy despite the fact that I was bloody, wet and hungry. The moon shone through the branches above the river, blessing the richness and crystal clarity of the water. The whirr of ducks' wings furrowed the air full of the river's aromas. I had to go to sleep and wait for daybreak, and in the morning I would immediately spread the story of my amazing catch in the greenhole near the Bulgie's.

Prince of the Una,

Dragons and Reconstruction

'The leaves have fallen and now float dead and heavy down the Unadžik,' I wrote with the terseness of a chronicler. I reread my words, observed the natural world and recorded the changing micro-structures of the river bank, the water and trees, when the roaring rainy backdrop of autumn gave way to the tranquillity of winter. Sometimes I headed off downstream from Grandmother Emina's house for no particular reason, just to check how things were. First, I would stop at our greenhole and look till I found the grayling; further down, in the shallow water, trout would be waiting; then there came a cascade, below which was another greenhole, where there were troutlet; then there came a stretch with a sand-and-tufa bed, where chub kept watch at Mita's house; further downstream the fish community was mixed; and just before the bridge young barbel with their golden bellies were in the majority, always clinging to the pebbles at the bottom. I was able to recognize and distinguish different fish by their traits. The appearance of a new fish in the aquatic realm of the Unadžik would heighten my passion of observation or, if you prefer, my obsession with fish, which required no logical explanation.

Wet and sodden leaves eventually sink to the bottom of the water like decomposed fish and become part of the river. The water loses its green-blue colour and turns icily transparent, heralding the long, cold winter. The whitefish withdraw from the Unadžik into deeper arms of the river, while trout, troutlet and grayling remain. Flies no longer fall on the surface, and the grayling now take only bread and the small crayfish from the bullrushes. The trout and troutlet patrol the water in search of small fry and become hungry and savage. Fishing for troutlet is prohibited during the winter and through until May. 'Troutlet' is our name for juvenile marble trout and they're protected up to a length of 80 cm, although hardly anyone abides by the regulation. The troutlet is a long, fast silver-white fish with occasional black spots along its back and sides. Its belly is as white as snow and its tough head is somewhat darker. It's one of the most voracious fish and attacks anything that moves in the water. Only the pike is more ravenous and has been known to snatch a full-grown duck, as well as feeding on frogs and goosanders – river birds that dive for small fish. Troutlet have a large white gullet, and in the late autumn and winter it's easy to catch them with a nickel spoon lure or a female butterfly with a fluorescent sticker that shimmers enticingly when pulled through the water. True anglers consider it a sin to go after troutlet at that time because they're blinded with hunger and attack every lure indiscriminately, but also particularly because troutlet are only a transitional stage in the development of the queen of the deep cascades, the Una marble trout, which can reach a weight of twenty-five kilograms. Several times I saw one of about ten kilograms, and I didn't want to meet a really big one in the summer, eye to eye, when swimming in the deepest greenholes made by powerful, foaming cascades.

The troutlet is the prince of the Una and its hunting activity marks the beginning of winter, which sheathes the river banks in ice and snow. Then the river is more beautiful than ever because it's decorated like a Christmas tree. The banks are coated with ice crystals of different shapes that cover the willow branches and bend them to the surface of the water. The water melts the ice during the day and the branches, whose bark has taken on a reddish, wintery colour, briefly come alive, but only till dusk, when the cold claps them in chains again. Once so much snow fell on the trees on the bank opposite my grandmother's house that the bank looked like one long dune of snow. They say the Unadžik only completely froze over once, sometime in the 1930s, and that it then resembled a Siberian river – a team of horses was able to go along it with a sledge full of children. People also talked about the river dragons that lived long ago in the hidden caves that the rushing

water had carved out of the tufa in the dark depths. The dragons disappeared many centuries ago when people gained mastery of the water. Or perhaps they're still hiding in their caves and only rarely, at full moon and under cover of the Una's unreal mists, do they fly out over the water and shower the river with gleaming scales. But enough of those empty stories.

The roof of my grandmother's house was like a thick, white layer of snow and ice. In the attic, the smell of dust and dry cobwebs covered the discarded objects. The floorboards of the upper storey gave a homely creak. The stairs in the short hallway were steep and you had to mind your head going down. There were narrow strips of space at the side, where rows of my grandmother's shoes from the time of the *belle époque* lay on old newspapers together with a box of Radion washing powder. When night fell, I would suspend my breathing so as not to wake the others in the house and would sit down by the radio. If I turned the dial to the left, the panel with the names of cities lit up. I got a special kick when a city with a curious name came up: Delft (I bet it's the home of elves with green caps, or dwarves that delve). I'm convinced I could sketch the house and the town with words down to the finest detail, but I have to be deliberate and taciturn, for I am the chronicler of a lost, sunken, incinerated age.

The Gods

of the River

When the water is angry, it rises up and turns the colour of milk chocolate. Thick and dark, it churns its way down the channel, producing huge whirlpools, and one glance at them creates a dread of the water's relentless flood, a fear of drowning and returning to inanimate matter. No one likes that colour because everyone from the Una tends to look down on sluggish flat-country rivers with their turbid water.

'What kind of river is it when you can't see the bottom?' we would say disparagingly of lowland rivers.

'There must be a terrible, murky secret hidden in those depths,' we continued, as we tried to fathom those thick and languid flows.

The floods usually come in the spring when the abundant snow on the surrounding hills begins to melt and the water comes rushing down, bringing a mass of mud, twigs, branches, and leaves and dead animals.

'Is the river up?' one angler would ask another.

'Yeah – and so muddy you could plough it,' the one who saw it first would reply.

River up, in fact, was an established local term for the great, wild flood that the Una becomes once a year, when all eyes are riveted on the water level with only one desire: that it return to its previous level and take on its Renaissance colour again, which is so hard to describe. When the water drops, its colour changes, becoming a brownish-yellow, then yellow with shades of green, until finally it goes as verdant as the winter wheat that peeks from beneath the snow thawing in the March sun.

The river has its gods too: the gods of depth, force, speed and colour. Dearest to me is the god of colour, so elusive to the human eye that adores and worships him with every blink – a merry and cunning god who constantly changes garb to match the riverbed and the sky above. The small fish enjoy him most because they dive through him and often take him as their protector when hiding from predators. This god is a lofty and benevolent demiurge, who in the Illyrian Age was called Bynt, a variant of the Roman god Neptune. There is no one who hails from near the Una who isn't able to stare into the river for hours. When I look into the water I forget my own existence and feel incorporeal, light and bewitched. Legend says that Roman legionnaires gave the river its present name when they arrived at its banks and stopped to marvel at the unknown water: they called it Una – the one and only. But I like to think it has always been called that, since the very genesis of the world, when it first began to flow. In the time when fish and birds talked with the grasses and listened to Bynt's calm, somniferous babbling.

Aquatic
Catharsis

How I loved the rain when it started to lash the water. A raindrop crashes into the surface, which then sends it upwards in a back-jet like a fountain. Thousands of raindrops bounce on the river, each creating a little circle that for a moment looks almost like a water lily. If the rain is heavy and fast, the back-jets seem to join with the river or to spout out of it and shoot off into the sky above the heaped-up clouds.

'Pouring from above and below,' Grandmother Emina used to say as she cleared out the ash pan of the stove with her tongs.

Rain can beat down with such rhythm and force, if only for a short time, that the opposite bank completely disappears before your eyes. And the river is covered by a watery curtain from which it emerges a few minutes after the shower like a milky white mist. The willow's leaves cannot be seen through the river's cumuli, but I know that when the mist disperses the greenery will begin to splash in all directions.

In my Grandmother's kitchen the piece of elecampane root on the stove smells of warmth and innocence. The Una takes on a pale-yellow hue that rolls down the river along the bank rich in yellow clay. A calm reigns briefly after the downpour, perhaps of the kind there will be in paradise, until the nightingale proves with its song that it is truly the heart of the tree.

The river is born again after the rain, and within half an hour the clay colour has gone and the Una returns to its old appearance. Plants that the shower bent to the ground straighten up and continue their eternal watch. When the sun, a god even stronger than Bynt, begins to beat down, the last traces of the rain will vanish and the droplets on the leaves will be spheres where rainbow children live. The first anglers' caps have already passed along the street that faithfully follows the river. Wooden windows creak and people lean out to breathe the town's loveliest smell – the aroma of the Una after a summer shower.

'She's clear!' they call out the old river greeting, and the extension rods protruding from the anglers' rucksacks look like antennas.

I leave my Grandmother's house and go to sit on the sandy bank. Sometimes I'd like to be a boat of leaves that, like most of the Balkan rivers, ultimately joins the Black Sea.

Although I'd never inhabited the body of a slug, I thought I could sense their sorrow as I sat there on the bank of the Unadžik and threw pebbles into the green water. But as soon as I caught sight of a sizeable grayling, my heart would begin to beat faster. At first I would just watch it for minutes, but then I would run back to the house for my fishing rod and tackle. The pleasure of outwitting and struggling with a fish so preoccupied me that I wouldn't notice when night fell. By the time I became aware of the crickets and the warmth streaming along the bank, bending the herbs and grasses and flowing between my legs, the full moon would have cast anchor above the water. The sounds of that riverine microcosm were a cradle for indescribable happiness and deep dreams in my Grandmother's house.

Grandmother

Grandmother Emina loved Comrade Tito, an atheist, although she was a devout Muslim and prayed five times a day. Her husband abandoned her and the three children she gave birth to in the railway tunnels where people hid from the Allied aerial bombing raids. The Second World War was over, and he went off to Banja Luka chasing the skirt of a certain Jagoda, at least that's what family oral history said.

It was beyond her to hate socialism, although the Partisans had executed two of her relatives under the dubious accusation of collaborating with the enemy. My Grandmother's whole family, without exception, were Partisan supporters. Grandmother herself, then a clerk at the local court, helped the resistance by carrying messages in her beige handbag, and her cooperation with the communists remained a deep secret. Therefore she derived no material benefit from it after the war. Many years later, only her cream-coloured shoes with the black, rounded ends reminded her of the time when she took messages from one prison cell to another in a miniskirt and with her handbag under her arm. That would happen when she climbed the steep wooden steps up to the attic – where she kept her old shoes – to put laundry in the washing machine, or to go to Uncle Šeta's room, where she would prop her elbows on the windowsill and watch the Unadžik for hours, looking even further, past the willows, through the avenue of aspens, all the way to the end of the aits, where the Una returns to one channel and continues on alone, without islands, towards Jasenovac. The husband who left her had been at the concentration camp there for two years.

My Grandmother didn't lose hope when her husband was interned at Jasenovac. On the contrary, she travelled by train to Zagreb, down the Una line that faithfully follows the river as far as Kostajnica, and tried to save him from the death camp. By plying several high-ranking Muslims in the government of the puppet Independent State of Croatia, Grandmother succeeded in having her husband released from the camp after he had been there for two years. Before that, according to family history, he had been interned for six months at the Stara Gradiška concentration camp, which is mentioned in a song: 'Jasenovac and Gradiška – the home of Max's butchers.'

Grandmother's husband survived the murder-sprees of sadistic Croatian commander Max Luburić and the slaughterhouse of Jasenovac. Her insider contact saw to it that her husband was transferred to serve in the Croatian Home Guard, where he was given the rank of captain on account of his university education. After a while he deserted the Home Guard and went over to the Partisans. My Grandmother was known to possess perhaps even mystical powers, and her inner strength exercised a powerful suggestion on people she spoke to, who would do what she said without reflection. That was our explanation of how she managed to rescue my grandfather from Jasenovac.

Like every true miracle-worker, my Grandmother never spoke about her powers. She used to say that reality was a toy in God's hands and that people were aided by Allah, to whom she prayed five times every day from when she was eighteen. 'Man proposes, God disposes,' she would tell us.

Imagine me now very small – so small that Mirdal Terzić can carry me in the straw shopping bag that smells of fresh bread and milk to my Grandmother's house in the suburb of Pazardžik. The first stop on our way was in Žitarnica, where we played badminton. Or rather, Mirdal played badminton with his friends, who were the same age as him, and I chased after a fat bumblebee, trying to swipe it with my racket-rocket and launch it into space.

Workmen were demolishing an old house on the hill overlooking Žitarnica and throwing roof beams down through the trees that had seeded at the edge of the cliff. The beams broke branches as they fell with a loud rumble to land behind the row of sheet-metal garages near the substation and the public toilet choked with vegetation. Mirdal told me to go and catch one of those beams in flight. I ran towards one that was falling in slow motion and then felt Mirdal's hands grab me before I could carry out the suicidal mission. He stuck me into the shopping bag as punishment, and my head looked out of it and swayed in time with Mirdal's steps as we made for Ustikolina. From there one could see the river islands, the football stadiums and the confluence at Ajak, where I later once secretly bathed in the early spring: I dared to swim out into the river's opaque green there, grey-hued from overnight rain, and only Sead saved me from drowning. It was April, and the water was high and freezing cold. Fish could be caught with angleworms. After that near drowning, mortality settled into me like an old man into a freshly whitewashed flat with a view of the sea. My childhood friend Sead survived the war but was killed in an accident like many other hardened veterans in the first years of peace.

I saw smoke from my Grandmother's house and we went down the narrow stairs next to the Harbašes' house, where I loved to study the slimy orange slugs on the mossy wall in the early mornings, before the world of adults took on its contours of earnest. Back then, the world was created anew every morning. Buildings fitted together again at right angles, roofs came down to land on the houses, and double windows returned from their cosmic journeys full of frost from having been at altitudes of over ten thousand metres. Willows, elders, alders and aspens sprang up again every morning on the banks of the Unadžik. Točile and the other hills rose up out of the ground on the fine line between night and day, taking up their established geographical positions. At night, bed is the only thing that's not an illusion, and if a person were able to be awake and asleep at the same time they would see myriad people in their beds slowly floating towards morning.

I got out of the shopping bag and ran down to the sandy bank below my grandmother's house. I saw the fish in the water: grayling and trout. The river bank smelt of herbs, grasses, bullrushes and the sewage pipes sticking out of the green bank, and I breathed deeply of all those aromas. The fish moved about, nervously and timidly one moment, then calming down and waiting in one spot for a long time like sentries. That was my world: I was a fish adapted to life on land – living proof of Darwin's evolution. I was the non-missing link, a transitional stage between fish and *Homo sapiens*, although I looked perfectly human. What a strange passion it was that let me go hungry if only I could watch fish, even at dusk, when everything goes dark and the fish swim to and fro like black spindles, sensing the night, a time of agitation for animals and people alike.

My grandmother's house was stable, safe and indestructible.

I waved to Mirdal who was going back into town along the asphalt road that leads upstream towards the Old Town. Mirdal was also a magician. He taught me to love nature and all living things, especially lizards, snakes, frogs and tortoises. I wouldn't have known what to do with myself without him. I went into my Grandmother's house as if I was sneaking in with my shoes on, something strictly forbidden. My Grandmother was in the living room, kneeling on her sheepskin prayer rug and facing the floor, which was a little steep on the river-side because the house was gradually sliding down the sandy bank. I had to go along with my grandmother's peace because she was miracle-worker and at the same time a paragon of modesty who never boasted about her powers, which made them flourish in my fantasy even more.

The whole day was ahead of me and I didn't know what to do next. Should I search for purple earthworms in my Grandmother's cellar, where discarded things have lain for time out of mind? When you pull apart a worm it has no choice but to reveal everything. Should I watch the fish and the movement of that incredible mass of water towards the Black Sea? Or should I sit on the wooden bench under the quince tree to smell its flowers and the plantago and wild chamomile?

The Origin

of the Species

On the last day of the school year we would go round to the western side of Hum Hill with our satchels full of jotters and textbooks and, just above the quarry, get down to the ritual of celebrating the end of lessons. That side of Hum supported a stand of Cyclopean pines, which grew even at the very edge of the cliff, and from there we would throw paper aeroplanes and rockets made from pages torn out of our jotters. We competed to see whose would fly furthest towards the far boundary marked by the blue curve of the Krušnica, whose banks were thick with long waterweed – swept with the flow of the cold water like the combed hair of a buxom nymph. Our legs dangled down into the abyss, its stony terraces covered in dust and gravel, and we half expected Old Shatterhand to appear on one of them with his horse and sweat-beaded brow, surveying the green hills of Govedarnica and Zalug with the keen eyes of a seasoned frontiersman.

We made our planes to be like Russian MiGs, and they really flew far away towards the Krušnica, but no one ever got one to go all the way to the river, maybe at most to the asphalt road, which created warm thermals. The asphalt melted in the sun there, leaving foot and tyre marks and indents of horseshoes. Although our rockets were aerodynamic and had pronounced tips, they flew very poorly and would quickly become unstable and start spiralling downwards nose first, a form of flight called the corkscrew. That was how birds fell from the sky when hit with buckshot from a hunting rifle: beak towards the ground and spinning around their axis.

At the bottom of the quarry there were hills of small stones and tired, old machines for the separation of gravel and sand. Puddles brimmed with slime, tadpoles and clutches of frogspawn that trembled in the tepid water, and the heads of small adult frogs peeked out of the green algae at the pools' edges. All burned in the midday sun and took on the sleepy, dusty, time-worn appearance usual for Mediterranean landscapes away from the sea. We couldn't see the Una from where we were. It flowed behind Hum Hill, and one of its arms joined the Krušnica there. The Krušnica was the most placid river in the whole area, deep and icy cold, because it was only six kilometres long. It emerged from a sheer rock face in virgin forest and was guarded above by circling eagles – the condors of our climes. After plucking apart our jotters and launching many a squadron of MiGs and paltry rockets, we'd settle to throwing stones towards the Krušnica. A stone could really fly far before it stabbed silently into the river and made rings we could barely see from our elevated position. Of all of us, only Duda was strong enough to throw his stone all the way to the Krušnica, and we held his marksmanship in high esteem: at closer range he could hit a mosquito in the left testicle.

High up in the pine trees there lived a special species of bird, rare and exotic: they were crossbills, and hardly anyone could boast to having seen more than two or three of them in their lifetime. Crossbills are members of the parrot family and named because of their beaks: the tips of their mandibles are crossed, unlike those of other birds, where the upper and lower parts of the beak are in alignment. In our hierarchy of birds, they were up on Olympus, ruling the avian world. Because they were invulnerable we declared them immortal, since no one had ever found a dead crossbill. When their hour of death came, they probably travelled skywards until they became just tiny dots and then they would disappeared entirely, to alight in some deep-blue paradise where they would forever be free of the physical sufferings of flesh, blood and feather. Free like ideas flowing through the expanses of outer space.

The universe is assumed to have originated as an idea that grew and grew, taking in lesser and weaker ideas. In the beginning, the 'Great Idea' did not have a material form, but over time it acquired a tangible dimension when it became pregnant with the weight of its own sounds and words. A primordial soup bubbled and

seethed within the Great Idea. The sounds and words had to free themselves from the parental embrace because every being seeks freedom and solitude. In this way, the planets, constellations, comets and asteroids were formed. P + planet, A + asteroid, M + meteor – everything was just named, and a sound would then join up with the thing it related to. Sounds made love with their meanings, and the universe was a colourful balloon.

But then the Great Idea outgrew itself and life emerged: Thrae was born, a tiny reflection of the Great Idea, a fragment of the one and only word, and it began its own independent journey, during which it became lush with vegetation and mighty oceans formed. And it flew through space so fast that an inversion occurred and Thrae became Earth. Life developed its own free forms in the jungles and oceans: primitive beings, animals, plants... and inquisitive humankind – the cardinal error of the Great Idea's cosmogony. Humanity's greatest infelicity is its material worries, and from its very inception it has strived to return to an incorporeal state like a miniature, happy idea. Just like the crossbill high up in the pines.

The Final
𝓑attle

Sunday. The day that convinced me that nothingness exits. Sunday was like a red trumpet playing into the ear of a weary, half-deaf colossus, and he scowled because his boredom was already so deep. Such an agonizingly slow day couldn't satisfy people like me. Even so-called workdays were boring for me because other children did what their parents told them, so they had no time to come out and play. I hated it because there were no children in the streets and yards. All living things were so tired. Sunday was a boon for the idle, and everyone holed up to rest. Respiration was reduced to a minimum and the movement of the eyelids were decreased in order to save physical energy. You could smell the tawdriness of the one-party system from the kitchens: bean stew without meat, and pickled peppers. Workers' flats were a cold, forbidding world, where nothing at all happened but everything was shrouded in a veil of secrecy and contemplation after the abundant afternoon meal. The knives, forks and plates in the kitchen sink were medieval weapons and armour dented after the battle.

In the absence of any human beings in the street I had no choice but to play with the stone.

It came from the moon, but I declared it a Martian because the red planet was much more appealing to me than the moon, which satellite images showed to look like a face pock-marked by craters of severe acne. That red circle, according to questionable mythology, was also the birthplace of the Roman god of war, muscular Mars, who today only takes the form of a silent statue in chilly museums. The gods of Hellenic antiquity, who by historical relabelling became Latin gods too, are all brooders and say nothing, according to the philosopher Heraclitus, who didn't want to believe Homer's poems with their frightening, human-like deities. I always preferred the Norse gods, with Odin at the fore, to Zeus' hangers-on, who were green-eyed and moronic like ordinary people. I loved the imaginatively drawn, fantastic Scandinavian gods from the *Stripoteka* comic magazine, who possessed formidable powers. Thor, the God of Thunder, was my ideal.

The Martian was on show in the china closet in Grandma Delva's living room together with Turkish-coffee cups of fine porcelain and crystal glasses for drinking cornelian cherry juice, which Grandma made by squeezing the pale red fruits in a wooden press with her strong hands when guests came. The alien was an irregular-shaped cobalt-blue stone with handsome white stripes; its edges were so sharp that you could even cut paper with them. It lay in that place of honour behind glass like a petrified mind, gathering invisible dust and waiting to be touched by my hand. As soon as the pads of my fingers came into contact with it, it lit up like Aladdin's lamp and started to hover in the air.

The living room was dark; the smell in the air was somehow stern and cold. Short-pile Bosnian carpets hung on the walls above the ottoman, their arabesques showing monstrous plants and geometric cities where the right angle was supreme. Shades reigned here, while the blazing sun beat down outside. Grandfather, a former Partisan wounded in the leg on a distant battlefield in Serbia, rested in the bedroom while Grandma, in the summer kitchen, rolled mince and rice in young vine leaves. The shades that reigned here obeyed me and told me hushed stories of the netherworld, of plantations where clumps of darkness grew instead of bolls of cotton. I learned the language of the shades while looking at those walls, where they would write their curt, quiet words. The shades most liked summer nights with a full moon. Then they were free and came from the netherworld, becoming human spies – spitting images of what every person will change into one day. If you free yourself of your shade you can become immortal, but no one has managed that yet.

The Martian shone with a metallic glow. The shades darted across the walls, colliding and merging like swift divisions from a twilight realm. They fought a battle, but no blood was shed.

That whole army ought to be set in motion and led out into the light of day to take the outside world in a glorious charge. May the light bulbs be little suns for people in their homes, and may the moon, twilight and semi-darkness endure outside. May nightingales sing a nocturne from one night through to the next, because day no longer exists with its vulgar light shamelessly exposing everything before it. Then all the stones from the moon, Mars and Venus will come flying. They will radiate a dampened energy, from which the shades regain their transparent bodies. And what about people? you ask. What will become of them? Let them be smaller than black poppy seeds, because all living things will be more important than them, and because their states and empires will dissolve in the long hexameters of nocturnal birdsong. Such was the mood that reigned on Sundays – that day that introduces us to nothingness.

Night-time
Journey

If it rains on the eve of Friday, the rain will fall for seven days, Grandmother Emina always used to tell us. And rain covered our sky with the force of the ayahs from the sura Al-Qari'ah (The Calamity).

I dreamed that the water surrounded us on all sides, and my Grandmother's house set out on its first voyage. Before we became Una-farers there was a mighty crash as the house tore loose from its earthly roots. Thus relieved of its foundations containing remnants of bomb casings and stabilizers from the Second World War, detached from the stones of the former house that burned down when the Allies bombed the town, and freed from the fluvial tufa at its base, the house prepared for the worst: a journey into the unknown.

The fleet-footed ones who weren't caught unawares by the water, like we were, climbed up to Ravnik on the very top of Hum Hill, where they hoped the sun would finally break through the clouds and stop the deluge. Those of us who had little choice and didn't want the freak weather to decide things for us took fate into our own hands.

Miraculously, the cellar retracted into the house and became our machine room with red pressure gauges and small, round wheels for steering in those precarious floodwaters. The valves of the gauges flipped up from time to time to let off angry steam whenever the engines ran hot. The grapevine uncoiled from my Grandmother's house and became a sail of leaves, in case other forms of propulsion failed. We tore through the deck with the help of a crowbar and I took up the metal steering wheels. My Grandmother stood at the kitchen window together with Uncle Šeta, who had served in the Yugoslav navy. The house had become a vessel and the kitchen was now the bridge, with my Grandmother as captain, holding her string of prayer beads. The amber beads circled in their silent universe. Šeta held a harpoon at the ready in case he spotted a giant pike. Water sprayed in our faces and surged towards the kitchen, but that didn't diminish our mariners' resolve.

We floated on down the Unadžik straight towards Pilanica, and all the way to the confluences, whose sandy beds always harboured barbel and sneep. Here the Unadžik flowed into the Krušnica and the two waters came together. The Krušnica stayed close to the right-hand bank, so the water was colder, while the Una took in the left-hand side of the fraternal stream. When the river was low during the summer, shaggy bullrushes would float in the middle of the current, and their flowers looked like the eyes of timid, pygmean hydro-beings. I tried casting a brass spoon lure made for use in turbid water through the cellar window, while closely monitoring the manometers with their red needles and following the course given by my grandmother. Skilfully, we steered clear of the thick, opaque layers of tufa that the water flowed over.

'Hard left!' my Grandmother yelled, and I would take the rudder and turn it until the house responded to the desired manoeuvre.

We were never in any great danger on our voyage, not even from the giant waves that collided with each other, creating formidable water giants. I recalled Nostradamus's verses about the end of the world:

At the forty-eighth degree climacteric
Fish in sea, river, lake, boiled hectic.

The river-side houses in Pazardžik had long disappeared from view and we passed down through the crests of the Pilanica cascades into the newly formed lake, which stretched all the way to the school and threatened to inundate the first houses on the grassy slopes at the rear of Hum Hill. Although it was the time of the year for floods, no one had seen one of this magnitude, at least not in my Grandmother's lifetime. Now we began to glide down the arm of the Una and the main current of the Krušnica, whose combined force submerged the long islands and everything on them for miles around. The crossbars at fc Meteor's stadium and the football pitch of its lower-division brother, fc Željezničar, jutted out of the lake showing just a foot or two of post. Mute, dirty water besieged the stadium's western grandstand. The bloated carcass of a cow hung in a goal net. Three hours from where we'd started, the water was trying to reduce Točile Hill by climbing higher than the crowns of the powerless trees. Birds' nests were swallowed up everywhere. Fish never seen in the daylight emerged from the depths, with ungainly bodies and heads so much like people's that some of them could talk.

One with tin scales called out to me in astonishment, gazing past my Grandmother's house at the clouds drifting above Točile: 'The first angel sounded his trumpet, and there came hail and fire mixed with blood....' Quick to interrupt it, I replied through the porthole of my machine cabin: 'and it was hurled down upon the earth. A third of the earth was burned up, a third of the trees burned up and all the green grass.' Upon which the fish withdrew into the silty depths, slapping the water's surface with its heavy tail. The look in its eyes was terrible – older than time. I thought I caught a glimpse of the Monster from the Juice Warehouse riding in a giant freshwater mussel and carefully noting everything that happened. Weariness was taking hold and it was impossible to ward off dismal thoughts.

At the forty-eighth degree climacteric
Fish in sea, river, lake, boiled hectic.

At that point the dream was cut as if by the blade of a Solingen knife and I woke up breathless in my Grandmother's guest room under the massive quilt. The beating of the clock's mechanism on the wall above me lent a Gothic note to the sleeping darkness. The house was still on dry land and the Unadžik back in its suit, which had not become too narrow for it. The water was content and travelled tirelessly on towards the confluences to mix with

71

the Krušnica's cold flood. I resolved to get up and go down to the cellar to check the red needles of the two metal water gauges, whose position and number showed the water consumption of my Grandmother's house.

I got out of bed at dawn and went into the corridor. Water was trickling down the coat-rack mirror on the left near the front door and the carpet in the corridor was soaking wet. The thick coats of white paint on the walls had cracked in places as if the house had been hit by an earthquake. Now I realized that my grandmother's house moved about secretly at night, nudged through the water with the furtive aid of aquatic protozoa and their cilia; its nightly progress could be expressed in centimetres, for the time being. Cilia are the tiny flagella of certain water-borne organisms, a substitute for legs. The house wanted to move to another, more stable neighbourhood, far from the wild river in my dreams and out of reach of floods and other disasters, to somewhere it could live to a ripe old age. It should be a town with better inhabitants – Peter Pan, Hansel and Gretel. But the house was naive, just like those whose hands built it. In the spring of 1992, the house thought it would be spared because it had never caused anyone any harm. All the other houses around it were blazing yellow torches on children's drawings. It made believe that there was such a glare all around because the stars had come out early in the sky. It pretended the other houses were not fiery suns that collapsed back upon their inner infernos. Its mind withdrew to the very highest point of the attic, where it cowered and shuddered like a freezing owl.

But all that the house had at its disposal were the cilia and the river, whose murmur would conceal its escape. Time flowed inexorably, and it wasn't on the house's side. The house prepared to betray its destiny, which has been repeated with horrifying precision every fifty years – that it be reduced to ash. Needless to say, its flight never succeeds.

Gargano, etc.

You will forgive me here for having to talk openly about the war. I know that's not popular today, but it seems that depressive visions of the future are. First you'll be fed and stuffed, and when you're up to weight you'll be ready for depression to be implanted in your herd-animal hearts. You'll mope through the shopping malls with your lumbering shoulders and fat arses, longing for the sirens' bodies on the hologram boards. They want to lure you into oblivion. They wear you down so your nerves are blunted and your chakras blocked, and then the future is here. Long live depression! That's why I've tried my utmost to block out the form and content of wartime images. I wanted to repress them and to push them under, like when you give someone a good dunking in the river by standing on top of them and forcing them ever deeper, down into the darkness at the bottom where the marble trout lie, until they run out of breath. I wanted to be like the unimpaired, conventional guys – normal and grey. If I secretly opened my eyes, the snakes on the fakir's turban would hiss and flick their tongues ever faster and more wildly, which was the fakir's way of telling me that I had to rid myself of the form and content of those wartime ghosts.

So I flipped the finger to the futuristic landscapes of shopping malls and biomechanical palm trees on the shores of dietary seas. I refused to drink cocktails concocted to give eternal youth to my face and genitals. I said good riddance to neoliberal depression – my demons definitely didn't live in today's world.

You will be offered progress and prosperity in strictly policed states, and you'll pay for them with oblivion. I don't forgive or forget, and I remember everything. To write means to speak, to make speeches to an invisible audience – this is my little rostrum. I can see no other way of fighting for the right to memory.

Gargano's Story

I admit it: I'm phantasmagorically mad. During the day, I see the sun in the hot colours of the night. I yearn for sex with the darkness. In the evenings, I secretly fondle my wounds, and I worry what will happen one day if they heal. When the round lantern in the sky goes out, the stab-wound on my forearm opens. I got it from a knife in a street fight, protecting a young lady of the night. My wound murmurs with waves that cast themselves up on a pebbly beach, feeling every single stone. Pine trees smell of resin. Sea creatures break down on the shore, spreading the narcotic aroma of salt. The sea at night is peaceful. Naked human bodies float in it, and spindle-shaped plankton gather around them and sparkle in the froth. My wound helped me to see the sea as a grey monster that hypnotizes me with its bizarre colour and force – a muscle-bound, wave-tossed slab that swallows up every reality. The sea is now metallic grey, now the colour of rotten cherries when the sun sinks into it; soon to leave no trace except in the mackerel sky high above.

The wound on my forearm is also home to a malevolent second self: dark-skinned Gargano, with soot-black hair and fiery eyes. Sometimes we swap identities, but I don't like that because the world seen through his glasses seems even gloomier than mine. Gargano had a sadomasochistic attitude towards pets and other animals in childhood. He loved and hated them at the same time. Let us draw a line: he was more inclined to misdeeds than me. Once he tied an emaciated magpie to the branch of a plum tree to hang by one leg and then used it for target practice with carefully chosen, sharp-edged stones. The river flowed beneath the plum tree with its blue and green eddies. The leaves trembled in the wind, the green of the vegetation and water dazed him, and he had to really concentrate and aim carefully. His arm muscles seized up and relaxed with an unnatural tic, and his mouth was dry with excitement. He was completely focused and devoted to his morbid game.

'If I hit it in the head it will go straight to paradise,' he said calmly to his companion, who was also throwing stones.

'But is this really fun?'

Gargano hated birds and only had a certain fondness for goldfinches and titmice, which accentuated the beauty of their plumage in the spring. He liked cute, tiny birds that could sit in the palm of his hand. Just as some people prefer tall, blond and blue-eyed individuals, Gargano preferred pretty little birds. He was afraid of big ones – birds of prey and vultures, so he had to hate them to diminish his fear. Nor was he inclined to ugly, sickly birds or those in distress. The magpie evidently fell into the ugly category. The other boy at the stoning of the black and white bird was older and taught Gargano everything about fish, water and fishing. In the end, holding the string squeamishly with the tips of their fingers, they swung the dead magpie into the Unadžik to be devoured by the cold vortexes because water cleanses and can revive even a dead body.

'*Aqua fons vitae,*' Gargano pronounced cynically and watched as the water consumed the bird.

Since I have quite a few wounds that can only be viewed at night, because the night keeps secrets, we quickly move on to the next. The second wound contains the Amazon rainforest, and I'll survive there too after the crash of my biplane, alone in the damp vegetation full of dangerous and cunning wild animals. I am used to that and enjoy it. I am a master of survival, which is why I have so many wounds. They tell the most superb and exciting stories. But first I have to take a machete and start cutting a path through the jungle's hostile green to make my way out.

When I opened the third wound, Gargano was waiting for me there too, sitting at the bar and taking long swigs from a bottle of Jack Daniel's. On the inside of his lower right arm, with which he was holding the whiskey, I saw a tattoo written in Courier New font: '`All those moments will be lost in time, like tears in rain.`'

He wanted me, and no one else, to describe him in words and bring him out into the daylight.

That was the birth of Gargano, a cynical creature devoted to darkness and adventure. Not an angelic being, demigod or straight-laced zealot who loves the monotheistic, pseudo-moral, paedophilic image of the world. Rather, a cruel and clever malefactor. A Darkman. One of us.

And now, dear civilians, as previously announced: please take a deep breath, and may your peacetime hearts not quiver. Here is a word or two about the war and what came afterwards.

A Telegram from Dark Waters

I hadn't touched the Una for months. The most I got was a glance of it. The river flowed as if nothing had changed. Three metres beneath the surface, in the heart of a greenhole, the silence was inviolable. The fish went about their miracles, and the acoustic impressions of an artillery attack on the dot of noon don't reach them. The forces of nature are insensitive to wartime operations. The tree breaks in half when hit by a tank shell. It has no words to complain with.

The river was far away and I became a man of dry land. I had a hump for survival – an army rucksack – and a rifle as close by as a third hand. My name was 'The First of Ten', a clear allusion to the Borgs in the *Star Trek* series. Borgs are superior beings that formed by assimilating subdued civilizations on the planets in their path. They're humanoids with metal implants, beings without identity and personality. One should actually speak of *the* Borg, singular, because all Borgs are one. They have no individual consciousness, and all their minds are parts of one group mind. They're telepathically interconnected, and their ships are the shape of a cube and have no motor because they travel with the willpower of all the Borgs on board. The Borg is a perfect image of a totalitarian regime, worse than fascism and Stalinism put together. The Borgs' best-known phrase is, 'Resistance is futile.'

During the war we called people who were still devoted to the ideas of communism, or rather who couldn't break with the mindset of the former regime, or 'communards' as we called them, after the group. Those people couldn't accept that they were being shelled by artillery and an army they'd helped fund with their taxes throughout their working lives. The grotesqueness of their behaviour in wartime conditions made them like little, awkward Borgs, forgotten by their mother ship and forced to be independent, which is what they most feared. They were saved to an extent by the hierarchical system of leadership and command within military units, where they felt relatively secure. Some of them eagerly accepted the new ideas of complete devotion to the new totem of nationalism, but I couldn't take them seriously in that role because they were still people formed by the old system, and the "communardism" in them would only vanish with their death. It's a strange irony that the communist system developed an intricate web of hierarchies throughout the country although the tenets of communism expressly opposed any manifestations of hierarchy and class. Our communist society was full of small class differences and inequalities – the State hadn't 'died away' but was constantly pumping iron so it would never lose strength and would remain eternally young. The communards had a term for this: state socialism, which was supposed to be a transitional stage to the withering away of the State in the communist paradise. Any similarity with monotheistic religions' promise of life after death is far from coincidental.

I commanded a squad of ten soldiers. Everything becomes easier when you turn into a neat number, and that was of my own choosing. I wanted to be a number, a random figure. I wanted to find biological proof, a pattern in nature that would be my equivalent, like in Darren Aronofsky's film *Pi*. I wanted to be reflected in the eyes of a horned insect, the stag beetle, which falls into the water in the August twilight and becomes food for chubs as fat as human thighs. I saw mortar craters fill with rainwater in no time and become little lakes – biospheres for ancient life forms that are insensitive to wartime operations and the military logic of the human world. Volvoxes, amoebae, paramecia and green flagellates. Pieces of shrapnel in tree trunks coalesce with the fabric of the tree. Only animals are afraid of death, like people are. Birds fly away to safer, calmer places far from the front line. Dogs start to whine and behave like snivelling children before an artillery barrage because they sense the deathly silence that reigns in the several seconds before it commences. Then ants and humpbacked carrion beetles pour out of the ground. Shreds of human flesh showered over the meadow flowers reek of sulphur and gastric acid, while biblical monstrosities of clean air emerge from lairs and dens. Sometimes I think I can even see the bacteria in the air if I strain my eyes.

I see them teeming and moving in all directions, and that crawling is the purpose of their existence – Roman legions advancing and subjugating the chaotic nano-world.

I wanted to return to mother nature, but it wasn't like I thought it would be. We lived in the forests, in damp holes, and slept between the roots of trees, estranged from the life stream of nature that couldn't be silenced by the din of the battlefield. Sometimes a nightingale would welcome the morning in the mutilated branches and sing for us lonely sentinels. That would happen when a deceptive ceasefire reigned and the birds gradually began returning to look for their nests in the thoroughly shaken flets of branches and leaves. Then you could enjoy your all-night guard duty, listening to the sounds of the forest, like the stream that babbled in front of the line, with downsized tortoises floating in its meanders, and inhaling the aroma of fresh leaves and humus full of robust insects. Enjoying nature was of little use when the shooting started again because it only intensified the colossal melancholy, that discrepancy between the bubbling of life and the silence a man slips into when he gets hit. So my facial features became coarse on the forest battlefield near Biljevine, while my beard grew bristlier and darker. I felt a spirit bashfully spreading inside me. But 'spirit' is too grand a word, and at first it was just like a grain, small and unsure. Then it grew and expanded. My spirit learned harmony with my body, matched my arms and legs, and matured in the all-encompassing nightmare around us. I was living matter with a soul. I knew other specimens too – soldiers who didn't have a soul, but that's a different story. I hadn't touched the Una for months, not even with my fingertips. I went down through the courtyard, knelt on the river bank behind my grandmother's house and immersed my hands up to the wrists in the water; tiny barbel were swimming, as hungry as an army.

For me, reality is what happened in the message of the underwater telegram. This telegram. Some of the things in it are enigmatic. What I cannot perceive with my senses is perhaps not real. I know that New York exists, with its capitalist skyscrapers, which from above look like a cemetery for the rich. New York is tangible for some, but for me it's a transparent illusion, a drawing in the condensation on an aeroplane's window, or even less than that. If the World Trade Center towers had come down during the war, I would have thought it a good piece of computer graphics simulation. My soldierly mortality stands in contrast to New York, and here it's embodied in the simplest inanimate objects: an empty cigarette case, but equally the sprayed-painted blue of a plum. That's what makes life in wartime so sordidly exotic. When you die, your spirit can fit in a cigarette case with a skull and crossbones and the Harley-Davidson logo on the lid. I was brave, and young, and my uniform fitted me nicely. My death could have become pop art, but then again I was far from the lights of any big city.

At Biljevine I read *And Eternally Rhythm*, a collection of twentieth-century French poetry. Published in Montenegro, it was given to me by a relative staying in a flat that had belonged to a teacher of Serbo-Croat – the teacher had fled from the town where we were now refugees. I kept the book under the tool and ammunition bag on my chest, behind the rifle kit full of golden bullets. The coarse fabric and my breath separated the poetry from the bullets. Poetry was more real for me than any New York: it helped me survive. I memorized Blaise Cendrars's poem 'Orion', which he devoted to the hand he lost in the First World War:

It's my star
It's in the shape of a hand
It's my hand gone up to the sky
During the entire war I saw Orion through a lookout slit
When the zeppelins came to bomb Paris they always came from Orion...

The verses mingled with the rotor noise of a Gazelle helicopter that plastered our positions with guided missiles. The sound of a missile is a synonym for alarm, a racing heart and a cold sweat all over. Months became years, in which I didn't see or come near the water. I even forgot its colour.

Why deceive ourselves? It was cold and we were at the edge of the world, in such deep loneliness that it crept to the back of our eyes. Or, according to Alija Izetbegović, our 'melancholic commander-in-chief' in Sarajevo: it was hot and we were fuel in a machine that demanded more and more dead, a massive pool of victims, until we all, living and dead, merged into one messy ball. We would be as cosy in that mélange as in the womb – almost outside of the perceptible world, safe in the skin of the victim.

Still, it was good sometimes on Padež Hill when a fire crackled in the little sheet-metal stove and the unwritten rule of the night-time truce lasted outside. If you wanted, you could fire a burst or two over the top of the parapet, just to let the others know we were alive, which would frighten the dormice and make them shriek like new-born babies. Your firing would only rend the icy, night-time silence of the nameless forest. Afterwards you spread your horse rug and got into your sleeping-hole. You lit up a *Gales*, greedily drawing in the aroma as if the rising column of smoke was a fakir's magic rope that would let you to flee to Las Vegas. You then sank into a deep sleep like colourless water in boots and uniform, with your rifle within reach.

Traumometer

Let us assume that the present is a body of water of particular colour and depth and that our bodies are immersed in it. Every body submerged in water is lighter by the amount of liquid it displaces, according to Archimedes' principle. But none of us ever come up to the surface, except the mad and the dead. The weight of our individual traumas can therefore be measured by the amount of the present displaced by our bodies. Yet small cracks seem to appear in the present because of all those who refuse to accept Archimedes' Law – cracks that threaten one day to wedge our dismal present apart, and the amount of frustration (potential energy) generated will deliver the kinetic energy required for a new war. Or, what is more often the case, the cracks implode within an unconscious body. The laws of physics rarely let us down. One such *invisible* book of the dead takes shape all by itself in the death announcements of the newspapers, listing all those who kill themselves.

Bright *Nights*

I burned inside like Jan Palach because I was full of energy and nothing could fully satisfy me. *'I Can't Get No Satisfaction'* was pounding in my head. Only death, perhaps, could fill and inflate me with breath that would come spouting out through ghastly geysers on my face. Only death could consume me from head to foot and send me speeding towards immortality like a human projectile. Yet despite the attractiveness of death, I was also frightened of it. That's why I would survive the war: I knew how to keep my poise and control that self-destructive urge. I had to find a reason to live time and time again because the proximity of death was so appetizing and irresistible.

The sun shone through the leaves covered with transparent-green aphids. It rarely reached the ground, where brown leaves lay rotting in the mud and puddles. Imprints of soldiers' boots plotted pastel labyrinths, with our lives and deaths in the centre. Our camp lay between wet, forested hills in two valleys connected by gravel paths like spilled intestines. We slept in shacks knocked together from sheets of plywood, which we had hauled up from the Šipad furniture factory on moonless nights, afraid of being hit by a stray machine-gun burst of a lonely, drunk Chetnik sitting bored at his guard post.

The wind brought whiffs of shit and piss from the latrines on the sides of the hills, where fat white maggots multiplied in the slush. Mosquitoes slept like brooches pinned to the boards of those outhouses, satiated with our blood. A cow with deformed hips hobbled around in the large clearing where we used to line up for the flag salute in the mornings. Its meat ended up in the goulash we had straight before one raid. The flag with the coat of arms of the medieval Bosnian Kotromanić dynasty on a field of white, now grey and torn, hung from a birch pole. Its design was thoroughly unwarlike, and now it looked like a pauper's cape to wrap a stillborn child in. We wanted to set fire to the commander's shack, just so something would happen while hunger dictated our thoughts. One soldier took an axe to it and chopped off the corner. Another suggested we go to Jaziće, where there were huge ponds and we could try to catch frogs, but now we were on combat alert before heading to an unknown battlefield. We killed our boredom by playing poker for cigarettes, lying around or picking mushrooms. I forgot the taste of meat as the diet of watery bean stew and macaroni eroded my palate. The coming of evening promised fragile sleep, wrapped in horse rugs, which I never pulled up over my face. For a moment, an unattainable woman appeared in my head – thirty kilometres of darkness lay between us, while chaos was all around and so close. I would spend the cold, damp night listening to the workings of my stomach and the buzz of mosquitoes' wings. Beneath our sleeping shack, diligent rats were reducing the plywood to sawdust. I wanted to go far into the forest and scream until my jugulars burst.

Whenever I walked at night towards these 'barracks' that we thought of more as a dump or a prison, I felt I could see a huge light away behind the forest or the next hill. That light always came from the direction of my home town, which had sunk into physical and metaphysical darkness. But sometimes I also experienced this optical illusion – a kind of mirage created by my longing for the town – in other parts of the country where there were no towns or villages nearby at all.

But the light existed and shone real out on frozen, snow-covered fields, which the cutting night wind blew over as if tomorrow was Judgement Day. It could have been the stars, because sometimes there were such starry nights that every little twinkle was mirrored in the crust on the snow that our heavy army boots broke with a cloud of tiny ice crystals. It could have been the moon or the forest's aura, the energy made by unknown sylvan beings in their warm homes under the ground. Or perhaps it was the Una itself, emitting electricity to signal that not everything was irretrievably dead and lost after all.

The Black
Sabbath

'Let's hang out at the old nursery school a bit.'

'OK, let's go.'

Less than a month had passed since the end of the war. We were still nowhere near getting used to being back in our town – realizing we'd retaken it and were now meant to live there again as we did before. Everything was back to square one, and from there we were supposed to head towards the light at the end of the tunnel. What light? It was hard for anyone to say what that was just then, apart from celebrating life with excessive merriment, food and alcohol. That was an easy, all-purpose stopgap.

We set off in the dark. I didn't mention that the street lights weren't working because nothing was working. The town looked like a battered film set from a movie about life after the apocalypse. The darkness was intense and as thick as motor oil, like a vein of lignite we were forcing our way through, we – latter-day Partisans in a march of liberation towards the nursery school. It was at the foot of Hum Hill, close to the socialist-style primary school we attended, and right next to the Cultural Centre. The nursery school was built in a beautiful grove stretching up Hum towards Zapadni Vinograd, where long, dry grass waved like in the savannah.

If I stand facing Hum, the primary school is on the left, the Cultural Centre is in the middle – in front of me – and the nursery school is on the right in the wooded part of Hum. Far to the right is the town's Orthodox cemetery, which I was always frightened of. Moreover, the path leading from the nursery school to Zapadni Vinograd goes past a private family vault enclosed by a metal fence. I never remember the names of the dead there. I was terrified by the physical proximity of the morbid granite.

But their decay supported a wealth of carefree plant growth. Nature was so rampant there that for a moment I was seized by the heavy melancholy of the decorative carnations, flowering roses and trees with woody lianas, from which hung traveller's joy, that cobweb of the plant kingdom; it all looked strangely out of place in our austere continental climate, which not even the Una could attenuate with its moisture and greenery. This tropical melancholy was heightened by the Osage orange tree, whose fruit grew to almost the size of a football, a giant yellow-green pod with a tough and wrinkled skin, concealing a shell that couldn't be broken even with a hammer: a fruit we called *pipoon*. That fenced crypt with its crosses and slabs was to the right of the path on a steep site falling away towards the asphalt road to Zalug, and beneath the road was a row of houses and then the Krušnica. The graves of black granite and marble were terrible proof of the death and horror that awaited us. We would be confined in cold, geometric forms. Nature at that miniature cemetery was so wild and rank, with a taste of bitterness, that when I walked there I often felt I was swallowing soil mixed with tears, worms and maggots – the very stuff of melancholy.

We went up the stairs near the Cultural Centre. Busts of socialist heroes once stood alongside the railings, but in the darkness I couldn't see if they were still there. The birds in the trees hardly made a sound. Clumps of soil had been scattered over the asphalt, and grass was growing out of them. The mayhem of war has a deeper meaning: everything is relaxed to the extreme and gives rise to a new reality – the limitless freedom of the human body and mind.

There were three of us: me, Tiny and Blackey (the tough lass); the adrenalin trio.

'Is anyone in there? Is it safe?' Tiny asked me.

'There's that idiot who used to drive his little fiat around town like in the video game Super Mario,' Blackey remarked.

'No, the top floor's empty. It used to be for abandoned children, and below the Chetniks held Muslim civilians taken captive at the beginning of the war.'

'Still, maybe it's best we not go in. Who wants to sit and drink in that Chetnik calaboose now?' Blackey argued before tipping back her bottle of Badel brandy.

'Look how strong I am,' Tiny quipped, gripping his jaw with one arm and trying to lift himself off the ground. He weighed no more than sixty kilos, without his uniform and weapons.

The tape in my head for recording events was blank for a time and I can hardly remember anything except a fight down in the cellar. I don't even remember the words that sparked off that nebulous event. We smashed bottles against the black walls of that former prison for Muslim civilians. The walls were thick with soot over the white tiles. The torturers had punctured the walls from the outside and stuck woodstove pipes in through the holes. Then they calmly sat and stoked the fire, like fishermen who have set deep trap nets and are just waiting for the fish. The smoke went straight into the cellar to the prisoners. The Chetniks called that group of civilians and the single soldier interred there The Mötley Crüe and accused them of fictitious criminal plans: a massacre of Serbian children with *Serb cutters* – metal spearheads and arrow tips from the Illyrian Age 'discovered' by their propagandists at the National Liberation Struggle Museum in Jasenica. They also staged a rigged trial in the first days of the war. The Mötley Crüe breathed in all that smoke in the nursery school turned torture chamber. When they were on the verge of asphyxiation, their former friends and neighbours – with respirators over their faces to conceal their identity like in a porno film – would open the door and lead them out. After months of this maltreatment, they were taken and killed in secret locations. Their executors remain unidentified to this day.

To cut a long story short: we had a raging argument in there, broke more bottles and got into a fight with each other. Afterwards we made up by talking about our favourite cartoons and nicely cut ourselves up. I scored my face with a flat piece of glass from the bottom of a bottle. I was the ringleader, and I really wanted to rip myself open. 'The captain leaves the ship last' and crap like that, but when it hurts any saying is just a heap of useless words. As blood dripped from my brow into my eyes and spread over my sooty face, someone socked me in the jaw with an iron fist – a Transformer with the physique of George Foreman. Tiny slashed the palms of his hands and Blackey her forearms. *We were here*, Blackey wrote with her bloody finger in the thick layer of soot and added an autograph: *The Templars of the Bosnian Army.*

The Layers of
Fear Inside Me

In the boy's imagination, fear is a creaky robot that walks the streets at night and indiscriminately chops people in half. I'm not that boy – I just heard him talking on television. On the contrary, I'm enamoured of robots, as well as androids and spaceships. I extrapolate the boy's imagination: the creaky robot dismembers people and gulps their arms and legs with relish. It roasts the corpses on a spit like Polyphemus. Human tallow drips from the spit into the fire, causing flare-ups and hisses.

Mr Fear's voice is the crying of a stillborn child. He is that metal menace, whose glowing eyes demonically splice the night, and the world becomes a raster in all the shades of black. That universal fear, both mine and the boy's, sometimes grips me in the stairwell at night, whereas during the day it's hidden between mouldy stacks of firewood, in rubbish bins, and down among the rats. When I'm lucky and someone turns on the light in the stairwell, my fear subsides like a fever passes. The front door of my block is a dark chasm – a yawning abyss between me and the door of the flat. I would call on the street lamp to help, but what use is that if it can't budge? The shield of luminous words is still incomplete in my imagination, so I can't take it outside. I stand in front of the building as if bewitched. When I finally manage to overcome my fear, I climb the ten or so stairs and I am quickly in the safe territory of our flat. It's warm there from the wood I've put in the Emo stove, and the little tongues of fire dance behind its glazed hatch.

The street lamp sheds a crippled light. The five luminous plastic spheres are arranged in a flower shape, but the resultant rose is maimed because one of the spheres is missing. We once used to smash them for fun: we would take a stone and coat it with clay, which we smoothed and squeezed until it was round and hard like a perfect snowball. Then we took aim at the plastic spheres of the street lamps. Boyish foolishness and disrespect for the material world.

The street lamp opposite my block of flats sheds a crippled light. I watch it through the window where bent figures of people go up into town along the empty street. It's late autumn, and the first snow delivers the final blow, from which it won't recover, although its departure has been well announced by spectacular fugues of red leaves rotting at the height of their power.

The credits and cast begin with the shiny metal sculpture of a knight on horseback turning on its axis, then my Grundig TV begins to show a *Survival* special about the African national park Etosha: lionesses lie around drowsily, crocodiles roll with wildebeest in their jaws at the watering holes, and birds lazily lift off from the tops of the acacias.

One purple earthworm is my time machine. A few words are also essential for the journey. I pull the soft worm apart as much as I have to so I can see its internal organs, and then I rip it to shreds. A mighty taste develops in my mouth, the taste of soil. When I speak that last word, winged phonemes lead me away to a land I've prepared for myself behind tightly shut eyelids. I depart the grey world of flats, slush and horseshoes clattering along my street with a tedious rhythm as if I am living in a Charles Dickens novel.

Then I fly through the purple wormhole. My body whistles and I am completely content.

I land at the foot of the giant grass. Every blade is the height of my block of flats. The flowers are like football fields. The caps of the mushrooms turn red and the spots on them create cheerful, simple enigmas. The law of this world has eradicated unhappiness. Short grass grows at the foot of the giant grass and provides a road, which my feet gladly tread.

The insects are the same size as in our world. There is no food chain, and no one eats anyone else because everyone lives on the smell of the gigantic flowers and the balloons of pollen that drift lazily through the air. This is an unfinished world as in a bedtime story that the teller skilfully alters every night. New plants and animals are constantly being added to it, new colours and creatures. Reading Stephen Hawking's *A Brief History of Time*, I realize I must never be allowed to meet my antipode, that anti-me, and that if we did meet we mustn't look each other in the eyes, because both of us would then disappear with a massive discharge of energy in the air, like the explosion of a fireworks rocket. Apart from that, there is no other fear. Gargano is safe, deep inside the wound on my forearm, and there is no danger of us ever meeting because he is in my flesh, shut away beneath seven sutures.

I hang out with a green android. He sleeps in the pistil of a huge bird of paradise flower. His skin smells of warm, clean bedlinen from the days when there was only one brand of washing powder. The green guy has blue eyes and prehensile eyelashes that he can make flutter like wings. We don't talk at all. We communicate through our thoughts. Our words materialize in the air and last until one of us thinks up the next sentence. We get into long philosophical debates about spring, summer and the meaning of different flowers because every flower is the bearer of a certain emotion. There are so many flowers that emotions must be the stuff this world is made of. Greeny confirms my hypothesis as we stop in the shade of a leaf that comes down to refresh us with its stomata, emitting cool oxygen. At the bank of an emerald river I realize I've been here before long ago. This world is as close to me as the skin of my mother.

'That is the Una with its greenholes – little pocket mirrors, in which Paradise sometimes looks at its face. That river makes life doubly sweet!'

In my thoughts, I almost shouted that at the top of my voice, with as much force as to shake the magic landscapes of orange-hued Micronesia or cause spots behind a person's tightly shut eyelids. But I stifled that desire.

It was winter on the opposite bank and I caught a glimpse of my antipode there; he was bending over and warily dipping his hands into the water, and then his arms up to the elbows, while gazing at the transparent blue surface. Perhaps he saw the contours of my face in the water's depths, down where the bullrushes would gradually lose their chlorophyll. Our movements weren't attuned because my antipode was in a different time bubble. I had to open my eyes and go back. Opening my eyes took a lot of willpower – but there, I did it!

The street light has gone out. The television screen shows a Yugoslav Radio and Television test pattern accompanied by a monotonous tone. The scent of Mother Earth fades from my nostrils. The phonemes are without enchantment now. The earthworm has been sacrificed. The pads of my fingers are stained with its insides. I've returned to Earth. I know it by the blood on my fingers. Blood is unpleasant, who's ever it is. The bathroom is ice-cold and the water washes the earthworm's tiny erythrocytes into the basin. The dirty water vanishes in the vortex of the plughole and returns to the Una: here it's lapped up by an underground giant, who lies horizontally beneath the river and the town. Don't ask how I know about the giant, I just do. He's lying down there and resting. When he turns over in his sleep, the earth trembles gently. Nature's cycle of water and fear continues.

2007

According to Gargano

When Gargano called me, hastily tapping in Morse code on the inside of my skin, I knew it was something serious and his tongue was just itching – he needed to confess.

I have to talk to you, town, because you're always present in my memory, and it is the only paradise from which I can't be expelled, the poet says. You're now a phantom town and your name is insignificant. You could also be called Zyx, but that wouldn't change anything for the better. Your dwellers walk the streets stooped and in constant fear of the weather's whims, of the sky that often changes its mood over the decisive days from the end of May to the middle of June. The favourite topic of idle coffee-house creatures, pensioners and young men is death in all its facets. Death comes from above and bears people away regardless of their years. It takes them up to the hanging gardens of heaven, among the concentric circles, thrones, divinities and cherubim, so say the holy books.

Death is your most developed industry and here you're peerless.

You're now a phantom town. As soon as swirling, coal-black clouds darken the horizon, everyone hurries home, as if home was a sanatorium where they'd be safe from the hysterics of the climatic behemoth. Winter is even more disconsolate because other monsters reign, formless and impalpable. There's no sun then, and no rain or summer storms, only shadows gliding through the town, the souls of the dead and souls of the living mingled in disorder and driven by the same restlessness; that feign anxiety spread by subterranean waters.

Winter is a state of limbo, whose every cell is made of depression. Those endless twilights that begin as early as half past four in the afternoon and have a pale and weak sun, unable to warm the sullen face that watches the outside world through a window.

Those nights, devoid of all magic because the minutes and hours are hammered into the heads of your dwellers like heavy-duty nails, puncturing their memory with its pining reminiscences of that other life – a former, old, better, more beautiful life where we were all young, strong and unburdened by others' death, memories continued in peacetime even when the war had ceased. Death is the only continuity that hasn't been disrupted. Such thoughts work their way along people's mental pathways in the nights as boring and eternal as the panting of the undertaker's assistant digging fresh new graves at the town cemetery.

Once you were different. They used to call you Little Paris. You were full of greenery, shops, bars, factories and throngs of people blithely celebrating the happy eighties, unaware of why they were merrymaking. People were as carefree as birds. If someone wanted to be poor, that was their own choice. Enjoying life came as naturally to you as the realization that tomorrow will be a new day. Your three houses of worship (with the Orthodox cross, the Catholic cross and the crescent moon with a star) stood so close to each other that you could sometimes see their shadows touch and intersect in the semi-darkness of a summer evening – a fantastic interpenetration of the earthly and the otherworldly. No one took any notice of that back then because that harmony seemed a gift of forgotten ancestors and something taken for granted. People lived without history, and outside of history. The Cold War only brought temporary fuel shortages and occasional queues for fresh bread. Soon the days of restrictions were over and the future opened up, sumptuous and generous. Or is it quite conceivable that you were never like that?

You're now a phantom town. Your foundations rest in not-too-distant memory. You're now a town of memory. You have none of the otherworldly vibrations that gave people faith in the joy of life. Now you are just home to plants and animals. A river passes through you that no longer bestows you the fruits of its waters. You're now a phantom town: a waiting room of death, second class. But it's quite conceivable that both you and I are nothing but creations of a coincidental illusion.

These are just a few of Gargano's random thoughts that I caught in shorthand because he told them to me like this. Then he shot up a tree in two or three hops, with the agility of a wild man. He sat on a branch, clasped his knees to his chest and stared absently into the fibre of my being. His long black hair covered his forehead. The leaves on Gargano's tree changed colour like a chameleon wanting to merge with its new environment in fear of serpentine predators. When the leaves began to bleed and the tree started to sob and shake uncontrollably, I closed my wound by passing my hand over it without touching it. I had to go out for a walk to break my own stagnation. I had to tear myself away from Gargano and his contagious thoughts. It's an awful thing to feel as if someone is tattooing you on the inside, on the walls of your internal organs. That's why I cried as I walked briskly through the empty evening streets.

Somewhere in the
Earth

I lay in Mother Earth in a field where we had dug-in facing the Autonomists from the break-away, north-west of the country, and my thoughts wandered. Above me were stars, below me churned-up soil, whose smell stopped me from sleeping, so I strung together sentences in my head to calm me. A cow mooed in its stable in an invisible village behind me like a mournful tugboat. The stars had no smell. At one point, they began to fall into patterns and jump at my eyes.

Let us enjoy the defeat of the sun that sinks through the deep-set windows of bewitched buildings, where old folk sift their loneliness playing Patience all day long. How can we enter the sun in the tally of these days? It is a pale mirror image of our faces, from which the solar paint acquired over the summer is now peeling. We are sun-loving vampires, and soon autumn will come – the time for deep sleep and lethargy. We bid you farewell, o sun, o great guest, o pygmy pentagram, as you fall into shadow on the other side of the globe.

The walnut tree's leathery leaves have withered and its fruit rolls down our streets. The sweet cores rattle inside them. The poplar is still strong, a secret home for goldfinches with their cheerful, pretty songs. One nest is level with the glass balustrade on my balcony. Inside there are two lovers.

Grass, that most amazing plant, continues its growth by the millimetre. Nothing can foil its intention of provoking the sky with its colour. Shrews cast up new and ever newer mounds of clumpy soil, which languid underground spirits rise from in the evenings – nameless essences, whose task is to refresh the air with the smell of loose black earth. Pears, badly bruised from their fall, emit alcoholic fumes, stupefying the day that becomes ever more tired and soon retires to sleep. Drunken, drowsy night saunters through the orchards and spills black ink lavishly in all directions.

The hills are gloomy in the evenings and a heavy aura of dampness and cold gathers over them, blanketing the point of life – the water vapour that forms the atmosphere. Birds rest in the branches and their fast pulses, like mainsprings, tick away a time unfamiliar to us. I've always wanted to burrow to the core of the hills, the heart of the mountain: to pass through the soil as if through water; to hold my breath and move beneath the grass and the tree roots, ploughing through the soft, carnal black earth; to bypass the living rock that is an island in the sea of the rolling, trembling ground. Perhaps only the dead asleep in their graves penetrate it, with the phosphorus of their bones lighting up their way.

The river is full of chub and their dorsal fins peep above the surface. They seem to want to leave the water and start walking on land. Chub are reckless and slightly stupid fish that will eat anything, even little berries that drop into the water. Early autumn is most certainly the time of the frivolous chub.

People, however, become worried and stern. They dream of southern seas. They put on thick, felted coats to keep out the north wind that scuds over the river, roams the streets and works its way into homes warmed by beech-log fires. The windows whine in the gusts of the north wind. For me, that is the dearest music of autumn's violins.

I will get up. Yes, I will get up and go to a cabin by the Una. I sing your praises, o autumn, o shaman of shamans that bewitches nature so as to strengthen it again. O perfect mechanism that rules matter, you mysterious energy – who was it that conceived you, named you and released you into the air, water, earth and fire? You are the air, water, earth and fire. The wheel of plants, the windmill of snakes' bodies and the fire of haze and mist are just a few of your visible signs. I heard an owl hoot, it too exalts you, while you drive the water that combs the hair of the tufa nymphs, brown bullrushes that rustle proudly and solemnly in the water's depths,

beneath which the spotted barbel spawn. They too celebrate you, the resistance of their bodies giving the water its fluid force. O autumn, luminous conquistador!

Lying in the trench, I dreamed of a man with fluorescent pimples on his face. When he started to foam at the mouth when speaking, the pimples would shine and bulge out like sparks on a summer evening. His pimples were dwarf stars. We buried that man because he had started to decompose. I sat beside his grave mound and waited for the fluorescent pimples to emerge from the ground. The cow mooed its deep elegy. Then they really did come out and gently rose into the sky. It was the black of night. I was lying in the soil of a battlefield. If an inquisitive Martian had been sitting on the jagged point of a distant star and looked down to Earth with his mind's telescope, he wouldn't have seen me. He would have seen the pimples giving birth to surprisingly large stars, as well as occasional, scattered bodies near the front line, in natural positions imitating death's calm: bodies, whose vapours coalesce into our dreams. I doubt he would have been able to understand things, even if he had exerted all his tremendous Martian willpower. The battlefield was a crude, hard fact, despite imagination that took me away to intact worlds of the forgotten past. The Earth was becoming warmer and warmer. The cow mooed its deep elegy. Tomorrow we would be burning houses and killing people with the same names as us.

1992

Year Zero

I used to know an old fellow from a nearby village who had been a tank crewman in a German armoured division and took part in the tank battle of Kursk. He was over eighty, short and sprightly, and he talked about the Second World War as vividly as if had just ended yesterday. He lifted up his shirt to show his belly and torso and said: 'See, I've been wounded all over. There's no place without a scar big enough to stub out a fag on. When the tank's ammo was used up, we jumped out and fought with knives. There were times when tanks crashed into each other, and the strongest came out on top.' Then he would take a long drag on his cigarette and watch the gentle May breeze rippling the green field of wheat. Through the valleys and over the hills came the faint rumble of explosions on distant battlefields. Just at that moment, one man was fighting for his life; another was already dead.

Do you remember Kareli? His house resembled the skin of the tank crewman, that tough old nugget. It was hard to find a single brick in the walls that hadn't copped an XXL piece of shrapnel. On the inner side of the wall, in the room where we rested after guard duty, an undoubtedly talented person had managed to find that brick and write with a flat, mason's pencil, in hindsight: 'Despondence and despair came over our boats, / The first days of war are fresh dew / And we are drunken bumblebees.'

Kareli was the man who ate a whole bicycle in front of Comrade Tito, as the story goes, and also several kilograms of dynamite. When they asked him how he did it, and if he had any after-effects, Kareli said: 'My stomach hurts a little bit, probably from the dynamite.' There used to be two Karelis – one in Serbia and one here. The encounter with Tito is attributed to the former, but for literary reasons I've ascribed it to the Kareli from our town.

His house – a huge, vacated human nest – was phenomenally indestructible. Although now as hollow as a cheese grater, no shell or missile could knock it down. We were safe in its concrete cellar.

We had been driven over to the left bank of the Una. The setting was the row of abandoned houses on the left bank, which lost all their warmth and original purpose as early as the second or third day of the war. The tenants fled and consigned themselves to being refugees. Their countenances were hazy and out of focus. Catapulted out of their own town, they would have to learn to be refugees in foreign towns and cities.

Although everyone with weapons moved fast and was always running under a hail of shells and bullets, everything now looked as if in slow motion, frozen as in in a wax museum.

One face particularly stood out in the general chaos: that of a young man in his early twenties with a scar and crossed eyes. His hair was dark but he had a fair complexion, with eyes spaced in a way that gave his face a slightly Asian look. His movements were energetic, and his body muscular and well built. His face was harsh and tender at the same time, a clash between the desire to look dangerous and his actual youthfulness. He stood with one leg on the windowsill and the other on a couch, looking out towards the other side of the river at our concealed enemy, who was armed to the teeth.

'Those are our local Serbs and their relatives from up on Grmeč. They've come down into town to settle old scores with "the Turks", he told me, still staring at their positions. 'That means us.'

Then he sneered at me: 'you don't belong here, you wimp. Clear out while you still can.'

His eyes roamed the room, which suddenly became claustrophobic because of the tension between us. Everyone wanted to be a hero, a lone wolf, because that's what drives the fantasy of young men hungry for excitement in war. Competition was therefore extreme, and at the beginning of the war every soldier imagined himself as an idol, about whom songs would be sung and poems written. The objects in the room were swollen from the damp and the parquet flooring played the role of waves at sea frozen by the movement of an omnipresent hand. The intact chandelier was

irritating, to say the least. If a seven-spot ladybird the size of a Red Delicious apple had come up and hovered near us, waving its little wings in slow motion, and started to laugh hysterically, the roof would have collapsed and the whole house with our tragicomic characters inside would have sunk down to the centre of the Earth, where Professor Oliver Lindenbrook, Lars and the pet duck Gertrude, evil Count Saknussemm and his loyal servant Torg were wandering aimlessly. But nothing crazy happened apart from the parquet cracking beneath our feet.

The young man's whole exterior radiated an elemental nervous energy and I was afraid to look him in the eyes. His face showed an abandon that had become ingrained because a large screw in his heart had come loose. That was the first and last time I saw him.

In 1993, the town we knew disappeared before our eyes. It was disguised by plants and ruins, and despite the explosions all day it acquired a hypnotic aura. We stared at it as if it was the last image we would take with us when we left this world. It became the strange, confused capital of that utopia we called 'I-want-to-return-home-and-for-everything-to-be-like-it-was'. There is something captivating in that decline that progresses from second to second. It affects the whole of material reality, and human works are the first to suffer: dead things become even more dead and break down into their chemical elements. Carbon is the most prevalent and dominates in ash to the same extent as in diamond. The destruction of Kareli's house reached its peak.

No one mused about water and fish any more. Anglers became warriors. In the complete transformation of one world into another, the leg of a pre-war footballer didn't kick a ball but had to take care not to tread on mines. At the end of April, nature awoke from its winter dormancy, and that went unnoticed too. Gradually we returned to primitive forms of existence, where the most important thing was to have a full belly and to be warm and safe. We learned to hate because that's the only way of surviving, and it can help unlock a strength and fury in you that keeps you alive and gives you the will to live. Learning to hate isn't hard, you just need to follow your body, whose impulses make you do whatever is necessary to survive.

We couldn't rely on an abundance of weapons and ammunition, nor did we have a mother country behind us, like our former Serbian neighbours did, so we relied on ourselves and what is strongest in a person: bravery. It was our deadliest weapon and helped make us into cannon fodder.

How ridiculous the desire is to come through it all physically unharmed. People do their utmost to get by without a scratch. They demarcate severe borders on their skin in order to preserve a heap of flesh and bone, a heart and, if they can manage it, a soul. They believe that the town cannot be destroyed, that it is imperishable. The streets are full of the skeletons of torched houses and new debris. Every little piece of rubbish has its life history and cries out for narrative reconstruction. One clump of rubbish is worth as much as Borges's *Aleph*, in which many different times, spaces, people, animals and things come together, except that their vital colours have lost their lustre like melted-down silverware. After that, the town and its people will never be the same again, assuming they live to see the end of the war.

Yet nothing will be like it was before, and this is a fact people are unaware of. Everyone believes in their own future and the potential of the town, which is surely how people think after every war. When our houses cease to be temporary museums making futile attempts to exhibit an untouched past, they will become habitable again. In ten years time, the outward signs of the war will be visible only in black-and-white photographs. Volumes can be written about the inner traces, but these will be pointless tomes that no one will read. It's a paradox that we were mangled in so many ways, and yet were condemned to win. This is a strange victory, full of the affliction of remembrance of the dead, the living and everything else.

The moment of vacillation and doubt passes, and I again believe in the town and the river: their strength and vigour will raise people up out of the ashes. They will give people the will to live.

The young man with the scar and crossed eyes was captured, had his penis cut off and stuck in his mouth. He has been dead for nineteen long years.

Snake

Power

We were doing a twenty-day deployment on the front line up at Sokolov Kamen. Nothing could happen to us because we were separated from the enemy by the deep and wide canyon of the Una, a perfect barrier that let us sleep peacefully at night and just demanded the odd patrol during the day. We went around bare-chested, collected berries, swam in a small dam, hung out with the Frenchmen from the United Nations, picked mushrooms and lay in the shade of the abandoned house. Snakes crawled about everywhere without interfering in our daily business; they were oblivious to the war and the shells that came pouring down. The Blue Helmets earned their pay by counting the shells that fell on our town, several kilometres downstream as the crow flies, and they couldn't know that we were getting used to the dead and all the ceremonies that implied. Over time, I went to so many funerals that they became a mechanical duty. Sometimes we would hang around furtively in the bushes, laughing hysterically, although a comrade-in-arms was being interred.

In the room on the first floor of the house I wrote convoluted, surrealistic poetry utterly unrelated to my surroundings. I was unable to penetrate the veil that obstructed my clarity of mind and precision of expression. That blockage made me launch a barrage of fiery metaphors from the Katyushas of my poems.

I didn't have a way with snakes like Emil the herbalist did, but I still liked them. They have a bandit-like streak and you can just imagine them destroying the Garden of Eden, home to Man and Ms Spare-Rib. Someone had to be to blame, so the snake and Eve were made scapegoats. Adam remained innocent. So I have to help defend the reputation of the snakes. They say that a fish in one's dreams is a symbol of worry, and a snake is evil and a sign of impending danger. But both animals are bearers of good news for me. The last time I dreamed of a ball of red snakes I won 250 Bosnian marks at the betting shop.

During a routine patrol in the summer of 1993, on the slopes of Sokolov Kamen, I saw a coiled-up snake, a horned viper. It was lying lethargically on a rock. I grabbed it behind the head and lifted it up. I don't know why, but I cut off its head with my switchblade and threw it down slope towards the Una – probably because it was wartime and I wanted to let off steam. Nothing much was happening at the betting shop, and I mainly backed number one; I rarely bet on number two – only in hopeless situations like when we fell into an ambush.

They shed their skin from time to time and leave behind a slough that looks like a cover for an antediluvian umbrella. Can you imagine such a hallucinogenic regeneration of life? You can't, of course.

A snake is absolute muscle with a gut running through it. If a galactic super-snake existed, it would be able to swallow and digest the Earth within a few hours. Death would occur immediately due to asphyxiation caused by the contraction of muscles twice the size of the Himalayas. I wrote a quatrain for the snake:

It comes from deep space near the North Star,
Riding a planet the shape of a skull
With fifty gleaming starlets on its brow
From the hellish ice where Muhammad sleeps.

A snake, monsieur, doesn't care for mercy. When I saw a grass snake patiently and persistently swallowing a frog the size of a man's fist, I realized what the face of God looks like – merry and mad. They're cheerful in a way unknown to humans, who mope over the civilizational jetsam they themselves have made.

When I was a boy, I was once garlanded with a large grass snake. The late Mirdal Terzić put it around my neck like a long, slippery piece of jewellery. I was as happy as a child-turned-king, initiated into the world of my elders, whom I admired, and Mirdal most of all. Mirdal, that magician from my childhood, the man with the safari eyes and safari hair, vanished one post-war day that smelt of oak in the dense pine forest up on Ravnik. Or we got separated for a moment in the savannahs of his safari eyes. He just went into the pine wood, which isn't so large that you can get lost in it, but, like a true magician, Mirdal knew how to vanish in the inextricable architecture of pine needles, to instantly soar up to the top of the tallest pine, from where he could easily climb onto the first cloud and leave our post-war world far below.

The skin of Mirdal's snake in my childhood was warm and supple when you stroked it. The gilded domes of cities, the illustrious peoples who made history in the battles of the nations, and the works of human hands from Leeuwenhoek's light microscope to the Hubble Space Telescope were third-rate rubbish when seen with its eyes – no comparison with a stone warmed by the sun.

But I was in a different state of mind when I stood on the tail of an Aesculapian snake with my boot, and its head was level with my mouth. I did this to impress a French lieutenant from the UN forces. He had come to inquire about our military set-up and told me I was a brave man.

'Pascal Rocher,' he said, holding out his hand.

'My name is Mustafa Husar – you know, like a hussar cavalry-man,' I explained. 'We're totally isolated here and fighting for our own reasons. We have no senior command and we're living on wild animals and what we can find in the forest. This is our line, and this is where we live. We are desperados.'

I was lying, of course, but there was also a grain of truth in the lie.

'I didn't go to military school. War is the best military school,' I told him, upon which he was forthright and offered me help in ammunition and food. That lanky Frenchman in a forest that looked so much like the Elven woods in the *Lord of the Rings*, with their mighty cover of oaks and beeches, gave the scene an underlying sense of reality – one that had fled from our dreams. If you want to survive, looking back is out of the question. There was no time for crying over pre-war life. It's good that limbo is devoid of memory. Our subconscious didn't function either, but we didn't need it. I wrote a quatrain for us:

The cold metal gun is a geyser of comfort
When adrenalin makes you touch it
It repels and attracts at the same time
So very similar to snake skin.

I released the snake into the tangle of ferns and grass. We were hovering above reality in an epic fantasy forest because there wasn't even a classical semblance of reality. We really were left to fend for ourselves, living on mushrooms and wild rabbit on the spit. Like a lost nation of Men in Tolkien's Middle-earth that has slipped from between the covers of the book, in the wilds below Sokolov Kamen in 1993. We were young, greenhorn soldiers imitating actions from the collective unconscious. That's why we and the snakes got on so well. Torture, killing, rape, pillage and arson are inscribed in us, but we can resist those untried capabilities. If you're ever asked for a nutshell definition of war, you can go ahead and say, 'It's like a double End of the World with whipped cream, only much, much better.' It's a plague of snakes the colour of the sun and the moon, and we make love with them all night beneath the open sky.

Emil

A long time ago, when the souls of our towns rose skywards like billowing clouds, a man called Emil lived and worked in our town. He was real, a man of flesh and blood. He was of Czechoslovak origin, and who knows what winds brought him here to the green valley of the Una, where a band of the ancient Iapydes people once decided to raise a village by the river, reckoning that its fruits would ensure them a good living. They respected the laws that the river imposed on them every spring without fail. They treated the floods as one of the elements. They would calmly collect their drowned livestock and the occasional unfortunate lad who had been reckless and got too close to the torrent, perhaps staring into a swirl that seemed to him like the eye of the god Bynt.

The Iapydes lived close to nature and rode to the banks of the river on oxen with branching horns, in which birds had woven delicate nests. Their decision to settle gave rise to today's town. It was here that Emil spent the last years of his long life. He was a man who understood the mysterious worlds of animals and could heal maladies with wild herbs whose names were not to be found in the compendiums of medicinal plants. But what he was most noted and respected for was his familiarity with snakes. He had a close and secret relationship with them. When people called him, he was able to go into their house and rid it of hissing reptiles. He needed no flute or other musical instrument as a tool for this unusual work. He would come empty-handed and make the snakes leave the people's home just with spoken magic formulae. The whole brood of snakes would obey and set off after him in line, and Emil would lead them away to a place they would be safe: usually an isolated rockery in the canyon of the Una. Elaborate tales were told about Emil, some of them true and others fabricated, as befits human imagination that embraces the whole world. Emil's skill was lost with his death. He was buried at the town cemetery in Lipik, modestly and with dignity. After several unprecedented rainy years, woody plants sprang up out of Emil's grave mound, and their tops were compellingly reminiscent of the ox's horns of the early devotees of the river. Those plants grew quickly and soon covered the decayed wooden cross, on which the letters and numbers of Emil's earthly existence had vanished.

Then Emil dispersed in several dimensions at once. In the dimension of hats, he was an island of purple, perfectly round and beyond description. In that dimension, you can buy a decent straw hat cheaply, for just a few kopeks. When you put it on, it starts a slide-show in your mind, and you see men of Srebrenica with their hands tied behind their backs – the whole process of execution in real time. The bodies fall to the ground and sink into it, through a filter of leaves and twigs.

In the verbal dimension, Emil was a forked, snakelike tongue at the court of King Revolutionaria. He was in the mouth of a corpulent snake that slept beside the throne. On rare occasions the snake, in discomfort and driven by an inner spasm, would open its mouth as if about to vomit, stick out its grey, forked tongue, and whisper: *Emil, Emil, Emil...*

The
Heart

One summer night in 1981, the Heart appeared on the prominent tower of the medieval Pset Castle, which was the pride of the whole town and thus merited its place in the coat of arms together with the river, which was portrayed in a symbiosis of blue waves with a waterwheel. The Heart, as we called it, because we had no other word for that enigmatic organism, tore stones from the dilapidated tower that went tumbling down the steep, unassailable bank of the Una. Those who saw it said it was huge and purple and beat so loudly that it made people dizzy and sent them fleeing headlong in panic. Others had different versions, from the one that the Heart was the united spirit of two ill-starred lovers – a local version of Romeo and Juliet, to the story of it being an alien that rebelled against Tito, the Party and socialist self-management. Others again repeated the belief that the Heart was a poltergeist created by the rage of warlord Matija Bakić, the last commander of Pset Castle, whom the conquering Turks threw into the river with his armour on. Centuries later, part of his anatomy had now come up to the surface and taken possession of his former fort. That's why I decided to climb the tower with its unsteady reconstructed wooden stairs to convince myself of the existence of the terrible Heart. When I started out on the worn, snaking path up the hill, with fragrant pines growing beside it, cuckoos in the trees betrayed my furtive approach and coo-cooed their autistic rhythms at the moon and stars. As I got closer to the tower, my own heart almost came into my throat and I shook and trembled all over. Sweat trickled down my jugular and I felt like a walking pine tree with sticky resin rolling down it. At the very top I was met by a breath of air from the river's canyon, turning sweat into starch and salt.

I caught sight of the back of a tall, grotesque figure. The terrified birds rustled in the branches.

He whipped around with a sudden spasm of his body, looked me in the eyes with his empty sockets and said, 'The first of the tribe is tied to a tree, and the last is eaten by the ants.'

Then he swiftly wrapped himself in his cloak and vanished in a whirlwind of leaves and dust. If I was God-fearing, I would have uttered a prayer, but I just stood there aghast, surrounded by the silent stars.

If the world is a dream dreamed by multiple, endless lines of beings who create it night after night anew, and if God, by a certain definition, is a circle whose centre is everywhere and periphery nowhere, then this night was an unusual vision that I experienced for a particular, but nigh-unfathomable purpose. Did the words I heard up at the tower only mean the doom of Márques's mythical Buendías or, together with them, the fall of the two easts and the two wests, the destruction of the continents and an attack from outer space, that was meant to herald a post-apocalyptic era and the coming renaissance there will be no one to sing the praises of? I have no proper answer, but the Heart didn't chill the hearts of the townsfolk any more. It faded into legend, the stuff of backstreet yarns, and I went on dealing with the souls of animals and plants.

Like every sensitive young person, I fell in love with high-sounding words like 'soul', 'brotherhood', 'freedom' and 'revolution'. I strove to be a picaresque poet, equally appreciating the brutality of the street and the enticing shades of the long, tall rows of books in the town library. Revolution! I couldn't wait for one to begin somewhere, and I quivered with the desire to burn in its flame. My wish would soon be granted, without me even being aware of it.

Spring

'Rosebud' – the dying word of the colossus played by Orson Welles in the movie *Citizen Kane*. It took me a long time to understand it and to learn the correct meaning of the English word. And so the time came for the budding of the trees' hardy branches. Spring always arrives like a rising tide, a green trance full of grasses and a whole mass of known and unknown plants. Spring is a religion older than Mesopotamia. I ask myself where the life spirit of grass go after it loses its green blood? Does it gather in some 'holy spirit' that bridges life and death? Are those minerals its secret weapons: water, ions, cations and nutrients to which give scientific names and chemical formulae? What were the driving forces called before we clad them in human language? What was grass called in the age before language? Or tree? I spoke *tree, tree, tree, tree* inside me until the word and its thought had become entirely dendritic. (Perhaps I sensed the meaning of matter for a moment, and perhaps I was able to touch it in my thoughts.) The letters were lost in that mantra too, the tree ceased to be a tree and turned into something completely new that didn't have a name or a mental image. It was as if you poured green ink into the air and then froze the passage of time. What hung in the air was impossible to describe: something shapeless and green that stubbornly refused to find its word.

It was that experience that points to human stupidity and ignorance – our horrible desire to explain everything for ourselves, to order and systematize things and then write a book about them, which will become a canon for fools who don't trust their own brains and emotions. Stupidity is epochal and unable to be reduced to a single root, and the whole of civilization is the outcome of it. Just look at the rules of grammar, that jungle of conjugations, declinations and phonetic mutations that sicken me whenever I think of them. Grammar is a playground for the petty-minded, those who start wars and tear the planet apart each century. Hitler is a classic example: he wrote a book and then put the content into practice. His admirers are exclusively people at a low level of spiritual evolution. Such tag-along killers are always in the majority, we can choose any time and space, the conclusion is always the same: the amalgam of stupidity and ignorance = mass murder. An intelligent monster is rather a recluse – it isn't a harbinger of evil and doesn't mix with those prosaic killers that populate its epoch.

'Spring is like a perhaps hand,' e. e. cummings portends for us. Spring is a carnal time, a time of convulsion. Every bud is the swollen vein of a many-eyed, invisible creature. Don't startle it! Walk through the vernal forest with discretion, when the song of elated, passionate birds accompanies your shadow. If you bend down to pick a cyclamen or a violet, take a look at the forest floor, the peaceful face of humus – it reflects your appearance more than any ancient books.

Awoken from my trance by a snap of fingers, with eyes open but still in a hypnotic sleep, I watched the seed of an Indian mango sprout in the fakir's hand and grow into a tree of natural size. I climbed up onto the stage and picked one of its fruits. The fakir suggested I eat it. Then he gave me a pencil and paper and asked me to write down whatever came into my head. That was the method of automatic writing I used to draft this piece about the spring.

The fakir's instructions were precise and clear. Using the technique of hypnotic regression, of returning to the deepest stages of my childhood, I surfed the experiences of my boyhood and teenage years, both ones I remembered clearly as well as those forgotten details buried at the back of my memory. There have even been instances where a hypnotist has been able to take the hypnotized person back five hundred years, to former incarnations. In a Copenhagen prison in 1945, a certain Hardrup met a certain Nielsen. Hardrup was serving a sentence for collaborating with the Germans. Nielsen introduced Hardrup to yoga and hypnosis, and also suggested to him that he would free and unite the whole of Scandinavia, but that he would need a lot of money to do it. After leaving prison, Hardrup robbed a bank, killing its manager in the process, but the court didn't acknowledge that he had acted under hypnosis and convicted him to life imprisonment with hard labour.

That was obviously a case of strong post-hypnotic suggestion, where a message is implanted in the mind of the medium, who, long after the end of the hypnosis, at the exact time determined by the hypnotist, carries out the particular suggestion, regardless of whether it clashes with the medium's own moral principles. I loved bizarre and insignificant events that had a meaning and a message; insignificant, that is, for the big history of humanity. I adored that parallel world of unusual people, to whom I belonged if only through my picaresque biography and the red scar cutting across my face.

I slipped back into my trance.

The Monster

from the Juice Warehouse

It was so long ago and I was so small that I find it hard to believe that it all really happened. I learned to walk and talk early and plunged straight into the whirlpool of life. Awake for hours before daybreak, I had to wait for the mechanism that ran the town's life to start ticking – and then I would rush outside. One morning when I was sliding between puddles, I slipped and fell face-down on the title-page of a wet newspaper clinging to the asphalt, where it said that Salvador All... had been killed (my hand had erased part of the surname). Allende was dead, and I was wounded. I kept running with the open wound on my knee and gripping the wad of newspaper in my hand. The day was a merry labyrinth that I wanted to get lost in, as in someone else's memory.

Maybe it was exactly the day when I crumpled up dead Salvador Allende that the Monster from the Juice Warehouse answered my persistent questions about how she could stand the loneliness of the icy caves. She gave a short monologue with a few allusions to silence, the cold and loneliness. I don't remember everything, but some of her words have stuck in my mind because I felt sorry for the Monster.

'I'd say silence is that feeling. *Gar-gar-gargel*. Silence floods over the hills where the green banners of the trees and the grass wave in honour of the watery power that nourish them. I don't see them, except at night when they don't show their colours because I dare not leave this shelter during the day. The silence isn't disturbed by the swarms of insects and birds but is enhanced by the holy melodies and rhythms coming from the very heart of existence: the fabric of the Earth or the astral spores – the meteorites that sowed the bacteria of life. *Gar-gargel*.'

Monster made these guttural sounds because her Eve's apple trembled uncontrollably on her thin neck, which held up a huge, melancholic head. I'd like to say her head was 'adorned' by unusually large eyes, but that would be dishonest. Creatures with eyes like that can never be completely happy. Whoever sees the world through such enormous eyes must have tears the size of Maybeetles. Just think how excited Monster must have been when a boy like me came by, and I was the only person she had to talk to. I stole adult books from the library and fed them to the insatiable Monster. You can imagine all the nuances of solitude that the well-read Monster from the Juice Warehouse reflected on as she sat in the cavern cut by human hands from the living rock, and upon which a medieval fort stood. And she had the even worse fate of being the last of her race.

'*Gar-gar-gargel*. Silence is easiest to catch over the surface of the water, and then it appears as a pale haze of river vapours rising elegantly like the spirit of a lady – a sovereign of aromas, elegance and tarot, with cards of tufa and sand. She is the Lady of the Water, who rules the water sprites and whose chill spirit brings evening calm to the houses by the river when twilight steals out of its heavenly chest full of worldly wonders. *Gar-gar-gargel*.

'Solitude can also be clad in cold, remember. Only that gentle cold has the strength to carry you away to the incredible dimensions and expanses impulsively produced by people's imaginations, imitating the power of creation we've discovered in religious cosmogony. Cold worlds, distant and untouchable, which everyone's soul longs for, exist in every water molecule, hanging in profusion like the cells of a honeycomb. Solitude is the possessor of the unique and varied atmosphere we get at the setting of the sun, and it resides in many words: gloaming, twilight, dusk, darkness, night, daybreak, black and blue-tinged morn, rosy-fingered dawn, eclipse, blackness... *Gar-gargel*.'

'Borges mentions two kinds of semi-darkness: pigeon-blue, that of morning, and raven-black, that of night. Solitude finds its garb in all of them, sometimes heavy like the cloak of a martyr, other times as gossamer-fine as the silk wedding veil that hides the beaming face of a mermaid, who will only vacillate between woman and fish for a few moments longer. Solitude is thus the strongest shield of sufferers and saints. They reproduce through it, confirming the purpose of their earthly existence. Life itself began because of the solitude of 'the one' infinite being. But what if solitude itself is that infinite being, whom the various religions have persistently tried to name and appropriate for themselves and their followers? Or what if it's expressed in the billions of feelers of eternity implanted in our bodies and those of fishes? One way or another, it's hard to make oneself clear to others and vice versa. That is solitude – an impenetrable protective suit of sorrow... *Gar-gargel.*'

While Monster was speaking, I had a visual notion of every word she said – my photographic memory registered every letter she spoke. I didn't understand the meaning of most of the words. I imagined solitude as a stalactite with cave water eternally dripping from it.

I drank my bottle of juice to the last drop and said goodbye to Monster with our old greeting: 'While there's juice, there's hope!' We knocked our foreheads together, and with thumb and middle finger we flicked the bungs into the darkness, where the Una flowed. Monster went back into the depths of the nuclear shelter, rushing for her bedchamber through tunnels where, four hundred years ago, the hunchbacks used to hide from people. I closed the steel door stealthily and silently so it wouldn't screech, then I dragged a willow branch behind me as I went to erase my footprints in the sand. I climbed the steep slope below the thick walls of the Old Town and walked in a zigzag over the grass to cover my tracks.

The town burned with electric luminance and the hopes and good wishes of its inhabitants. I went down to the asphalt road below the Catholic church and hurried to the old town fountain to wash the green palms of my hands. It was late in the evening and I joined the flocks of people out strolling. I already knew very well how to keep a secret.

PS

Monster, an envoy of the water and the aquatic world, according to her own tale, came into being because the powers in the sand of the Una sensed an influx of misfortune from the human world that threatened to spill over into the aquatic world. The demiurges of the sand united, and their combined strength gave rise to a powerful aura that emerged from the water, from which then strode forth an awkward and wistful human-like creature. Her task is to observe people and their way of life, to get close to them by reading their books, and in the moments before her death to convey that knowledge to her father-mothers, the demiurges of sand, who have ever been wardens of the river and its world. Thus the sand knows the history of the human race better than humans themselves. How can Monster prevent that onslaught of human misfortune, I hear you say? Very easily: by absorbing it into herself and then expelling it from both worlds through solitude. That's why she has such big eyes. And that's why her lifespan is very long because the elimination of human misfortune requires a lot of human time, and solitude. But since that misfortune accumulates at such a rate that nothing can stop it, the powers in the sand decided to stop probing the human mind. That's why my monster is the last of her sort.

I first met her long ago when I used to pass the storehouse for fruit juice, a cavern hollowed out of the bank of the river island where the Old Town once stood. Formerly people used it for storing ice, which was brought from the caves of the Grmeč range and then delivered from here to the various taverns and kitchens. The juice warehouse was, of course, a place for storing juices of all colours and kinds. Rows of plastic crates stretched as far as the eye could see, and the moderate damp and cold made it ideal. Strange noises always came from the juice warehouse, as if the bottles were murmuring and squeaking, bobbing and bumping against each other. When I went in for the first time, attracted by this music, Monster was standing behind the massive, half-rotten door. I was so small that I could squeeze in by pushing apart two loose slats of the high door. So began our friendship, which ended when I went to do my military service because Monster could only be friends with children. When I grew up, Monster disappeared, along with so many other things.

The Ballad
of the Black Hole

We all know that heaven is above and bright-burning hell is below. And God rules supreme on both floors. Between them is the Earth, where we are. And God is our master. Such is the order of things as imagined and inscribed by the paedophiles in priestly robes. O Man, you sacred beast! We warrior Adams are just ordinary animals in the vast kingdom of Regnum Animale. That's why I forsake myself as a man and would much rather be a whale shark, *Rhincodon typus*, fifteen metres long and as heavy as a bus – a gentle, mega sea-dog that eats only plankton. But I've mislaid the shape changer, so now I walk the town, whose architecture will be embellished by fire and made infernal over the next four years.

My town was a place where heaven and hell kissed. Shreds of mortar shells were raining down, bouquets adorned with bursts of 20 mm flak rounds. I ran and entered a large room of a damp, one-storey house. Through a hole in the ceiling and roof I could see the stars.

The moon lit up a photo portrait of a passionate pair of lovers with frozen smiles. She wore a crown of silk on her dark hair. His dense crop was combed back with more than a dab of brilliantine. They were lying naked on a bed with brass bars, caressing each other's hair and holding each other tight as if every night was Judgement Day. He remembered his birthplace in the marshy borderlands between Lithuania and Poland, and as a boy wading through the peatbog, up to his knees in the cold slush, touching in wonder the speckled eggs of a wild duck in a nest covered in leaves, and it trembled on the surface of the black water. His homeland was in those marches where *wind often changed the borders*. Or at least that's what I imagined as I looked at the photograph, which the damp and the sun had made ever more like a daguerreotype.

With her head thrown back, the woman combed her long hair in front of a framed mirror, examining the reflection of her well-proportioned body with its pronounced hips. She ran a finger over the rosette-shaped birthmark above her navel that brought her good luck. Every time she did that, a smile would make little wrinkles dance around her eyes. She let her hair down over her breasts, and the curls covered her erect, protruding nipples. The man lay on the crumpled bedclothes smoking in the dark. When he inhaled, the tip of his cigarette would glow, revealing the lack of one finger – the price he paid for fighting in the Ardennes. His gaze was fixed on the ceiling, through which the stars shone.

I leapt out of my mouldy bed in a flash and stared at the flare that whistled low over the roofs before going phut. The gunfire outside stopped like a sudden summer shower. Gunpowder was the Christian Dior of the nightly air. Sheltered by a row of houses, I walked along the street, which was about one hundred metres long and dead straight. There were quite a few unrendered houses here that hadn't been burned down, and the moonlight revealed the holes bored by shell fragments in the red brick walls.

Black holes hide in shrapnel pits
Small tight balls of raven feathers
According to Hawking, the light here is endlessly bent
Fly fervent into a wormhole and you will come out again alive.

I threw myself to the asphalt that had been colonized by grass and soil, and a flare lit up the half-burned houses, rampant weeds and the skeleton of the Alsatian Arkan, who had died of artillery fever. Have you ever seen a dog trembling while shells are falling? Arkan shook like a frightened person, and it was that completely human fear that killed him. Pale sprouts of grass now grew between his ribs, and larvae had lasciviously sewn what remained of his skin with the threads of their scabby bodies.

Half-burned houses are clocks with atomic precision, which show that the time of the war has only just begun to flow. Because when the heatwaves and the rains come, the fire-marked building material

will turn to debris, and the interiors of the houses will swell and pucker; winter will grip them in its freezing vice, and later they will crumble into dust and ash, becoming soil and returning to the earth over the years of maltreatment by the forces of nature.

No one lived in this part of town any more because of the closeness of the river, which was the front line. I felt that the whole street and all its houses were my possessions. Not a breath of wind stirred the trees in the courtyards of the phantasmal, but still real houses. My senses were finely honed and almost perfect on those lonely, night-time walks. The street was filled with my body, my sweat and the smell of my weapons. My innermost being spread through the forsaken courtyards and entered the houses with their broken windows and unlocked, half-open front doors. I felt the aura of all those desolate houses, their hidden warmth and the mayhem of war in their courtyards as if I'd spent my childhood in each one of them, although I'd never been here before. This street was the homeland of my first year of the war. Here I discovered my secret peace. The evening dew condensed on the weeds and the other colonizers. I thirstily inhaled their smell, bitter and pungent, together with the ether formed by the midday shower. A silence steamed from the street that was only possible after a fierce exchange of gunfire.

I would roam the town that night, borne by the wild freedom of my body, bristling with excitement because a shell could fall any moment and put an end to the story. My heart throbbed in my whole body under the camouflage pattern of my uniform. I enjoyed gambling with something bigger than myself. But it wasn't enough to say I loved life. I loved it so much that I was willing to die for it. Oh, sweet tenderness of war that drives my heart to explosion. And that wartime sky with Van Gogh ochre stars arched over my love for that unknown street is my salvation – only now do I know it – from the scourge of hatred and vengeance.

So I run along the empty street with my jaws wide open like *Rhincodon typus*, and heavenly plankton flows into my mouth.

If I were a Catholic, I'd proclaim that being torn between the desire for a normal life and the thirst for blood was nothing short of saintly. But I'm not a Catholic – I'm a member of a people that, in Bosnia of the 1990s, was earmarked for the same fate as the Jews in the Third Reich.

Refugees

Grandma Delva is a purple bird with clean, soft plumage. She walks tiredly, with a rolling gait, on our way home through Žitarnica. I take care not to trip her with my foot as she shifts her weight from one leg to the other, and I'm scared that the neighbourhood dogs and cats could dash up and pounce on the purple bird that talks.

I ask her if she's afraid of dogs and cats.

'I'm too old to be afraid of anything,' Grandma Delva says and waddles on, the sun shining through her feathers like a comb through hair.

Now we're right in front of Grandma's house. The front door is overhung with Mediterranean plants, some hardy, others luscious. Even now, that green rampart protects the three or four stone steps that lead up into the air, surrounded by black walls with weeds growing at acrobatic angles. Already during the war we noticed a new type of house that has a convertible-style roof. Although I know she's dead, that doesn't disturb me at all because I'm glad we're talking as we stroll through the watery strata of sleep. It's as if we want to compensate for all the words unspoken during our lives, when I was a boy and high-school student, and Delva a vital sixty-year-old with a white Yugoslavia filter cigarette in the corner of her mouth like one of the Immortals. As soon as one flagged, Grandma replaced it with a fresh cigarette.

'May thunder singe your socks!'

'Damn and deuce you!'

I hear her colourful expressions that once resounded behind the hedge, from the window of the summer kitchen. Its floor had an opening with a wooden cover. When you lifted it, cold and darkness welled up from below. Rungs met your feet when you went down, blindly, into that cellar with neatly stacked piles of chopped firewood. It smelt damp and musty – just like I imagined it would in the underground hide-out of my Partisan Grandfather and his

wife Delva, who came from Mostar. I don't know if this will make sense, but there was something very precise and soothing to that smell: if I breathed in deeply, I'd be swept away to a dense forest that smelt as if every tree was the essence of their underground world. The hard hats of fungi that grew on trees had the strongest odour, as did the moist forks of branches. The forest litter and humus smelt of earthworms, whose intestines were full of soil. Its aroma was strongly arousing.

Grandma Delva's plants were the only things stronger than the war. The suburb of Žitarnica diminished like everything else after the battle to win back the town. The way unknown plants grow at right angles out of the walls is moving. Here, where life has been scorched, there is fertile ground for new growth. Those rooms with neither floor nor ceiling can be launch pads for soaring up into the sky. Everything that was once in the house has done exactly that. Blackened and heavy from the smoke and fire, gasping for air, they found their way upwards. The rooms' coolness and darkness, the Bosnian carpets, ottomans, porcelain, crystal glasses, vases and cutlery, the tin woodstove, the light fixtures and the stone from Mars, or rather the moon, are now all immortal refugees.

Grandma and Grandfather are at the town cemetery in Lipik, alongside each other. Their souls have entered the map of stellar pathways. On evenings when the Leonid meteor showers fall, refugees returning to their earthly houses are skilfully concealed among them. Life is repeated in all its simplicity, full of little habits and human rituals.

'May thunder singe your socks!' and 'Damn and deuce you!' can be heard between the meteors that burn up in the atmosphere.

Indian
Summer

A warm October wind passed through our hair and swirled the grit and grime of the street. An unexpected energy took hold of us in those days when the putrid beauty of autumn accumulated in nature. It was a time for playing basket and ball, for active daydreaming and gazing into the starry sky, for adventures that wouldn't happen, but the thought of which would live on when snow covered the world in white impassiveness.

The plumage on the duck's neck shimmered in all the shades of the rainbow like the horizon in paradise. The weeping willow lowered itself over the surface of the river and greeted the millions of faces anxiously travelling downstream towards the kingdom of the tropical sun. The river spirits were troubled – eternal travellers who always changed their appearance, taking their cue from Proteus, the god of waves and tides.

What if memory is only a delusion, a system of perfect deceits arranged by the tangle of human nerves? But all this is real: a whole string of words to describe the river, and a river that wants to verify the world – our world prone to cyclical destruction.

The first video game in our town had a fantastic sound, and whenever I hear it in my memory now it reminds me of a different time: a life of innocence and peace beneath the bell jar of the Yugoslav atmosphere. Clunky, two-dimensional spaceships blinked statically on the screens of the hulking devices, usually near the upper edge of the screen, and our mission was to destroy them by firing puny space cannons, which were only able to cause slight exterior damage. The game was called Galaxy. You had to destroy the galaxy ship and beat your personal best score. That sound represented the cannon's blast when aimed at the ship. I wasn't all that good at killing spaceships. There were also other ships in the game, which looked like little bats with folded-back wings; they flew fast and erratically, dropping deadly bombs, but that wasn't a problem because your stock of lives, given in the upper-left corner of the screen, was still substantial.

As soon as you entered an amusement hall, as they were officially called, you would be bombarded with a mélange of sounds from different glass-and-metal boxes with pretentious English names, where cosmic battles were simulated, or a pinball machine happily gurgled in its electric language when someone won a replay. I was most attracted to the square glass case on metal legs, which contained packs of cigarettes with unfamiliar names imported from distant countries of the capitalist West. The glass case had a lever that operated a metallic hand with robotic fingers. That mechanical hand allowed you to pull out and win a pack of foreign cigarettes, and that was considered quite a feat because hardly anyone succeeded at it. Often you would pick up a pack of Rothmans with the metallic fingers and triumphantly start to move them towards the glass cube's exit hole, but the robotic fingers were crude and clumsy and the cigarettes would promptly fall out of their metallic grasp. None of us smoked at that age, but each of us longed to grab a pack of cigarettes and lift it out of its glass confines, to feel the paper in our hands and smell the aroma of cigarettes from the faraway lands of the capitalist West. There was something almost sacred about that. We yearned to touch that world of neon lights and the sleepy glare of the street, things seen only in American road movies – to grasp what was different and untouchable, which we faithfully imitated when we listened to electro-rock and new wave.

This was meant as an evocation of an Indian summer, a mood that spread over the whole planet like a radio wave – the story of an autumn and of a river that travels through itself. Then the organic gods of nature joined forces with the electric messiahs from the cumbersome, flashing video machines, which is possible only in memory: *Time takes a cigarette...*

An Angler's
Hymn

I fought with the trout for three days. It was my first experience of a struggle like that. I only drank a little water, and didn't eat anything for three days. Uninterested in the routine of everyday life around me, to others I seemed like a *Muselmann* from a Nazi concentration camp. I kept up the pressure at night, too, casting a fluorescent Mepps lure – that was the proper way and helped kill time, but the real fever wouldn't come until daytime.

My adversary was a brown trout. Back then the Una was still free of introduced rainbow trout, which are not particularly noble because they go for anything anglers throw at them. The aim was to catch an energetic, crafty fish, not a fat one you could hook just like that. A brown trout with red and black spots on its upper body and a golden sheen from the side-line towards its belly is a gem of the river. The shape of a brown trout is natural and fish-like, while a rainbow trout looks like a saw with fins tacked on.

My trout came from down in the tufa of the main current, slicing the cascades with its dorsal fin like a hot knife through butter, and the greenhole just below Grandmother Emina's house was now its home and hunting ground.

I watched it rule the deep like Captain Ahab's whale. Old and sly, it wasn't going to be caught easily with flies on the surface, which I cast out over the water and skilfully dangled the fly just above its mouth, in the hope that it would jump at the 'yellow drake', swallow it and churn up the surface as it tried to pull the line with all its strength towards the sandy bottom of the greenhole.

It missed the fly several times, and its powerful tail broke the smoothness of the water that flowed away with its own sense of eternity. Then I managed to hook it and drag it two or three metres, several times, but it always released the fly and quickly vanished into the safety of a shadow made by the sun shining on the tufa. My happiness would turn to bitter disappointment for a moment and I would become dispirited, but only until the next cast, when hope returned. After a few seconds of being on the hook, the fish would go livid with rage, or was that just a trick of the light and water against its body? Mosquitoes bit me and I was gleaming with sweat, but that didn't bother me because fishing is a passion greater that can be found among so-called vices. Some anglers find calm in their hobby, but for me it was pure excitement. Then my heart pounded with a cosmic rhythm, just as Élie Faure once dreamed of.

Next I tried to catch it with a small, live fish, which I fastened to the hook and cast with a sinker to give it weight and help maintain its balance as I drew the bait through the gleaming water. The trout snatched the fish and began to swallow it, revealing its snow-white jaws and pulling at the line, which I slackened so it could carry off its quarry wherever it wanted. When I judged that the small fish was on its way to the trout's stomach, I tugged the rod skywards and began pulling it towards the bank. I already thought it was mine, restraining my heart that brimmed with immeasurable delight, but right at the bank, with a rustle in the bullrushes, it freed itself of the hook, and the rod went straight and the net became limp again.

I spent all of the next day on the lookout for it, casting Mepps lures, flies and bait. But when I wasn't lucky enough to catch it, I just crouched on the bank and watched, and the pleasure of seeing its firm, fleshy form enchanted me, reminding me of the bright azure of the sky at full moon when it fell on the heart-shaped leaves of the grapevine at midnight. The leaves that beset the walls of my Grandmother's house like Gog and Magog.

When I finally caught the trout, I laid it on the scales my grandmother used for weighing icing sugar and flour for her cakes, and the needle shot up to 900 grams. It was a huge, motionless spindle, a silver sword adorned with red and black cockades – a trophy with absent glory and a glossy, greasy fin that circled in the sky by day and night, waiting for its shooting star.

The Smell of the
Burned Town

Our town grew out of people's bond with the river. The Una is the power that holds the town together, otherwise both the river and its people would have been swept away long ago; like tortoises with houses on their backs, they would have fled far and wide. All the people of this town are believers in the water. They know very well that most problems vanish by simply watching the flow of the river. That's why it's so worth living here and committing oneself to lifelong faithfulness – to the preservation of the secret union that must not be revealed.

Whoever marries the town ends up at the cemetery in Lipik or in one of the many family graveyards. The tombstones are testimony to people's love of the Una and its world. I once had a strange experience: I was walking through town, feeling all nervous; I raised my head by chance and caught sight of the gleaming white marble in Lipik. Immediately a sense of security and relief came over me because I realized I would be buried up there too – on the hill where an enemy tank was dug-in during the war, and where battered old tombstones were stacked in the loose earth before the war when the Mahala hospital was built over part of the Muslim cemetery.

We made this town, Bosanska Krupa, of black mire, yellow sand and green water borrowed from the Una. The tall towers of our town tickle God's feet. Then someone always knocks it down again and tramples it like a sandcastle, with painful nightmarish precision. The next day we would try to raise all those castles, Rapunzel towers, Gothic cathedrals, vivid Russian churches and barbel-eyed Ottoman mosques from the river sand again before the stomping giants came back. They always come from the north and head downstream, faithfully following the river. They're clad in mist, and the sun is a medallion on their chests. I trust that I'll be able to cheat fate by waking up before I'm crushed. The war descended on us just like this nightmare: without end and without a rational beginning.

I don't want to know anything for sure about the origins of the town, and I don't want to deal with stale old topics and be a doom-monger, because history has never taught anyone anything meaningful. The water knows, but it doesn't talk. There are lots of valuable records concerning the town's first rulers, the dukes of Babonić, and the founder of the town Blagaj on Sana, Babo Babonić, whose descendants were known as the Blagaj Babonićs. According to Croatian historian Radoslav Lopašić, by the late thirteenth century the Babonićs were known to be holders of huge tracts of land all the way north to the Styrian and Carniolan borders, and also far into Bosnia to the east, beyond the River Vrbas. Babo Babonić's son Stjepan founded the line of the dukes of Babonić-Krupski, and who is mentioned with his brothers Radoslav and Ivan as viceroys of Croatia from 1294 to 1316.

What I do know for sure is that everything repeats itself: history is repeated and the slaughterhouses of nations are renewed – they're never destroyed completely because their technologies are secretly preserved for reuse. Mass graves are a chorus through time, and towns never come off well. In every war, towns are the litmus test for the degree of the people's fury and destructiveness. All I know for sure about the origins of this town is that it is covered in a crust of bitterness, because history is an exhibition of graves. I don't want to remember all the repulsive things from the war. All I can say is that my blood is a contribution to this form of history.

Me, I still believe that our town arose from people's bond with the river. The town is a freshwater mussel with a pearl inside made up of the best wishes of its dwellers. That's my childish imagination speaking; when I'm old I might one day discover what the town really means to me and others, if that question interests me then at all.

For now, it's a haven by the water to which you can always return, even when you're thousands of miles away, because the thought of it is faster than light. It's both imaginary and real, and two-fold

like light. My sailing, literary town, older than the stars: I can only save it if I remember.

I was fascinated by the town when it was 'ruins in progress', with houses razed to their foundations and others half-burned, with fire-blackened buildings and bridges. You enter a house, and around you there are just walls, above you the sky, and in the kitchen there stands a fridge, intact and full of chunky maggots the size of macaroni. Timbers reduced to charcoal jutted out of collapsed roofs. There was mutilation and imperfection everywhere. Birch trees with their innocent, grey-white bark were already growing out of some roofs. Fire had cleansed the town, freeing it of surplus people and other living things. I loved the dirty streets criss-crossed with power and telephone lines, and covered with branches, leaves, scattered personal belongings and books that had tripled their volume from moisture. Disintegrating shoes, futile umbrellas (because the rain had turned to shrapnel), casseroles with carbonized food like those found in Pompeii, wide-open doors of houses, broken windows, facades as if a giant had bespattered them with mouthfuls of food – destruction seemed quite a natural state. Half-burned roof beams, which had been quietly smouldering the day before, now smell like smoked cheese. I even think I only really came to love the town when it was thoroughly in ruins. Not because I pitied it, but because its beauty spread outwards in radial waves towards all the continents.

The
Hunchbacks

They are seen in the twilight hours shrouded in mist and rags of deep-blue night. No one wants to meet them – neither the baker, nor the nightwatchman nor even the drunkard, who is afraid of nothing by then. The hunchbacks are all we have left from the last war. They are all that we are not: dirty, ragged and unrecognized members of our society. Each of us has their hunchback, and all of us are afraid of their outlines up on the town roofs that cast disfigured shadows, making the weathervanes' strutting roosters and golden angels look grotesquely alive in the night-time wind. When the day is fast ticking away, the wind lures the hunchbacks out among us humans, who pray to God and dream assiduously of the promised paradise.

Although we are aware of their existence and the smells that hang in the air for hours over the cobblestones together with the steaming droppings with undigested stalks of meadow plants, no one will ever utter their name. That is a secret we swore to keep when we came to this town of spirits, to the smoking ruins wreathed in eerie silence, like the desolation of a mass grave. It is not their name that is forbidden and untouchable, but a whole chain of facts that should be forgotten because we are alive, while they are more like the half-alive. They are in fact mostly dead, with only some traits of the living such as hunger, thirst and an inclination to nightly anxiety. During the day they hide in the catacombs of the town, where not even the biggest fool would stray. Our priest said that their name was holy, but also unspeakable, because that is what the Almighty ordered, except in prayers when it is proper and holy to name the causes of their emergence.

We inherited this town through unfortunate circumstances: the death of all its population. Half of them perished in the eddies of the river, sinking in the sweat of their armour and chain mail to the bed of the Una – into oblivion, not legend – when a mighty host struck on 23 June 1565 and razed Pset Castle to the black ground. Those who survived became food for the grey crows and ravens up at Ćojluk that glimpsed another feast in that town shielded on all sides by the river. It took us three days to scrub the stubborn blood from the pavement in front of town gates, where a handful of enemy heroes broke through our lines. But we soon cut down all four of them, while their commander, 'a mann of heavy bodie', drowned in the Una.

This battle won't be recorded in any major history books, but for the participants themselves it was very important indeed, especially for those who lost their lives.

We live here in our town together with the hunchbacks at the borders of the empire. We have sufficient food, ammunition and weapons, and our destiny is clear, as cannot be otherwise at the edge of a mighty empire: with constant ordeals and battles ignored by historians, with swords that became scimitars, and with a young moon above the highest tower of our invincible town.

Whenever the town is besieged, we withdraw within its thick walls and burn the bridges. We take our horses and cattle into the stables filled with hay. The river is then a boundary that erases the borders of the two empires, and we remain among ourselves on the island in the middle of the Una.

People are like birds – susceptible to the wind that brings varying voices. The main thing is for us to be calm and collected. An astrologer taught us to gaze into the sky, search for constellations and give them names to help us while away the long hours on nightly guard duty when only the river can be heard, and the cascades imitate the boats of a ghostly enemy. But that is only a trick of the senses we have long got used to. Fine snow falls on the satin roofs, and winter resembles a mausoleum.

Then I think how it would be to jump from roof to roof, light and elusive like the water sprite that comes out from below the Kožara cataract on those nights when there is a lunar eclipse that frightens the livestock.

The constellations have interesting names, which we pronounce in at least two languages. During sieges, our hunchbacks withdraw with

us behind the walls. No one mentions their stench and no one shuns their bewitching eyes. The hunchbacks know the tunnels through the rocks of the island that lead to fresh water and even better fishing. But that is not why they are now treated as equal members of our society. It is because of the war, and because we believe in our dead and like to think we will not become like them. It is because we are blood relations, and blood ties are respected in wartime. If we live out the siege, the hunchbacks return to their caves and are banned from the daylight once again. They are allowed to walk the town from midnight through till the crack of dawn. None of us have become sufficiently acquainted with their logic, even though the better educated among us speak at least two languages and can read three alphabets. The hunchbacks are a sin we dare not admit; I do not know if they think the same about us. Do they hate us or secretly admire us? Here on this river island, at the border of two empires, with armour that is closer to us than God... I will soon be dead, and my mind will be broken...

All this was written in old vernacular Bosnian on a tufa slab that I, Hasan the diver, brought up from below the Kožara cataract in the summer of 1999. The words, in cursive Cyrillic script, looked as if they'd been engraved with a dagger or sharp sabre, although that would hardly have been possible. Who could have thought that such frightful battles took place in and around our Old Town? As if for proof, I, Hasan brought up an Austro-Hungarian sabre from the riverbed. Its sheath was well on its way to becoming tufa, but when he pulled out the sabre, it blinded us with unimpaired radiance. Its wooden grip had decayed, but the silver wire that had been wound around it was whole. We were all afraid, standing exposed on the grass in our swimming trunks, when Hasan started to brandish that sabre.

Tonnes of water and sand overlie the fatal din of ancient battles. Fish live between the surface and the riverbed as if in a giant, God-given aquarium. Books are mute – they confirm nothing and are unable to revive the past. Plants cover the two prominent towers of the Old Town and the Una is beautiful and stubbornly silent, supporting the old assumption voiced by Borges long ago: that official history is just another offshoot of blossoming fantasy. The testimony of one anonymous person is more valuable than the coldness of encyclopaedias.

Diving into the
Mirror

The time of vibrant, disquieting pleasure begins. Summertime, when the sun's rays – the arms of a deity that accepts us, drawing us to its immortal, nuclear heart – will scorch us all over so we become as coppery dark as American Indians in Western films. It's the time for swimming, which begins around the First of May, because that holiday will be celebrated by the banks of the river, and the boldest and most inebriated are sure to throw themselves into the water and be baptized in the cold, clearing their minds and cleansing their tired, workers' souls. Meanwhile we children will hide in the secluded curves of the river, strip down to our white underpants, and enter the water with a shudder and slight fear of the cold, until the river turns our lips blue and our thumbs freeze from the pleasant cold of the greenholes and mighty cataracts.

Swimming is something people hanker for all through the autumn and winter, too. No one talks about it when it's snowing or raining and people's steps are sodden with the weight of uncertainty, but the desire is buried deep in our hearts and, like the bud of the quince tree, is just waiting to blaze up in an irresistible onrush of happiness and physical pleasure. It's about affirming that fine germ of life, which nothing can snuff out because summer has come, which is our time of year. Then people avoid work because the sun makes our bodies lazy, allowing our muscles energy only when we swim and dive down to watch the sand at the bottom as it swirls in the deep currents. Then you really can grab fish with your bare hands, except that as they are protected by a layer of mucus, they soon slip away, and bolt into the opaque, green veils of the river. It's hard in the summer to wait for the sun to come out and traverse its path to the zenith, so sometimes we meet at the river bank at nine in the morning and talk about the water, waiting for the sun to give us a secret sign that swimming can begin. Before that solar wink, we keep checking the water with our fingers and hands, comparing its temperature to yesterday's, and we always conclude that it's even warmer and more beautiful than the day before. When the first body finally jumps in, all things from dry land are forgotten. No one remembers the dusty streets of the town any more, nor the sweltering heat that turns the asphalt to plasticine, which can be sculpted by our feet. Worldly problems vanish as soon as you plunge into the water and set your eyes on the tranquillity of the riverbed covered with sand and waterweed; which exist as if nothing in the outside world is of interest to them. They exist only for themselves and the fish that will search for tiny crayfish and tender larvae there. The Una, that fluid, flowing oblivion, prepares us a long-awaited pageant.

Perhaps we really are reborn every time we dive into the water. We return to primordial caves adorned with seaweed; our memory returns there. Perhaps our cells remember their former shapes before the scales fell from our skin and we finally began crawling through the shallows towards the terrible dry land. Swimming was then another word for resurrection and new life. Oh, how we used to pity towns and cities that weren't lapped by waves of holy water because every body of water is sacred and magic, even a narrow stream that makes its way through the underbrush of a nondescript paddock. Our rivers elevated us in our eyes and we felt we were chosen and special compared to all the deplorable towns deprived of a water source, or in comparison with those that bathed in turbid and dirty streams, whose riverbeds weren't visible like this mirror of ours, into which we plunged every day that we swam. It's hard to deny that life arose from the water. The bond with the life-giving force of nature that we feel when we jump into the water is beyond comparison with other gifts of the earth. Entering the water and becoming one with it is that closeness that lovers throughout the ages have yearned for.

Green
Threads

I awoke with a jolt from my hypnotic trance, without any apparent external stimulus. A tincture of darkness, private and personal, was in my eyes. Immediately I wandered off into the dark, away from the leather chair, and panic sealed my mouth like a black billiard ball. I staggered on like a sleepwalker, feeling in front of me with my hands for fear of falling or hitting my head. This couldn't be sleepwalking because my mind was working flat out. Everywhere there were protrusions, holes and sharp objects. I expected to break a leg or get an eye poked out, but nothing of the kind happened. I came across a large puddle of sticky liquid. Adrenalin intoxicated me like backwoods hooch. My feet grew heavy and I plodded on like a defeated army. Who knows where I was, in what chronotope, because after some time in the dark hall I lost all sense of external time, and the space around me could have been a slavering maw. When I fell to my knees, my hands touched something soft very close to me. I recognized it at once: grass – fragrant and clean.

It's matchless. Nothing else has such persistence, not even the rain, which is tangible on your hands like sands of bereavement from the sky. I watch it breathing beneath the snow, and its colour assures me then even more of the permanence of this world, however much the sacred books try to convince us of the opposite. Even though grass is the unruly hair of graves, that cannot lessen its worth in my eyes. On the contrary, I shall consider it even more terrible and unshakeable because I know that one day it will conquer the world, leading the other plants. In fact, it has ruled the world since its inception as the silent vanguard of the vegetable legions.

In the beginning there was a green cloud. Then the cloud – *verbum caro factum est* – took physical form and came down to Earth. That body divided by parthenogenesis into a multitude of tiny life forms that milled and thronged over the Earth's crust. The age of grass is hard to establish. It existed long before trifling human things such as language and religion. Only with poetry, which is the 'alpha and omega', does grass enter people's concept of immortality. But I know there has always been an equals sign between grass and poetry. The last poetry will be made with poorly articulated sounds from the last throat. Then the wind will take command of the acoustic world.

Grass gives the world its essence; something not even fire can destroy. I watch it sprout and break through the crust of charred soil. Ruined houses smoulder and smoke all around me, muffling the echo of explosions. At first it's pale, later it becomes dark and serious in its persistence. The smell of burned earth has crowned it, and it ascends through the air in invisible ferry-boats. When I travel, I often want to stop and fondle the green hills. Just as a dandelion resembles a balmy sun to a two-horned insect that warms itself on its tender petals and feeds on its pollen – I, the traveller, am sustained by the colour of grass.

When my earthly term of office expires, I'll become a hardy blade of it, one among a myriad. I'll be plural and singular. Devoid of any elegy for the body or other fictional surrogates for sorrow, I'll be simple like you. And those who can make do without pronouncing my name shall have my blessing, just as I was blessed as I lay in the grass that towered up to protect me, as I inhaled the pungent aroma of its mowed stems, setting off a sensual rush of blood to all my extremities under the exploding blue of the sky.

A two-pound roach jumped out of the river just below where I was lying on the high bank of the Krušnica, watching the sky, and made me sit up in a flash. Fish sometimes come flying out of the water like that when chased by a large marble trout or a pike.

The Krušnica is a peaceful river with remarkable, constantly flowering bullrushes, which used to spread down the banks and

create the impression of a self-effacing archipelago. This was the favourite abode of pikes because they could easily melt into that tangle of bullrushes. A hiding pike there was like a tiger in a bamboo thicket. It may well have been one such lurking hunter that made the roach launch out onto the shore. The frightened fish soon returned, thrashing, to the cold water before my hands could grab it. The river drew clouds to itself with the strength of a magnet. The first drops of rain allayed the shuddering tension that spread through nature like an electric shock. The fish fled into the depths to continue their struggle for survival. And an impression of my body would remain at the place where I lay.

When at long last, God be praised, I came crawling out of that theatrical imitation of dry scrub, blundering through tufts of real grass, I saw a luminous object moving in the fakir's hand. I managed to find my chair again. His eyes were grey and cold, and his mien as clear as mud. I reached under the chair to check if my bottle of beer was still there, then I ran a finger along the red scar on my face. I trusted the fakir, although it had looked for moment as if he had forsaken me. Unlike most neuropsychiatrists, the fakir didn't view me as a helpless endemic species that had to be saved from extinction by stuffing it full of pills, whose trade names were reminiscent of distant stellar nebulae. I didn't want to float in An-Silan 3 and Indosin Balthazar like an insentient asteroid. Before the phase of relaxation and induction into deep hypnotic trance, I had forced myself to memorize a sentence: 'Through the cracks in the wooden door I saw dirty snow that the sirocco had shaped like a board for a coffin.' In my dream, I quickly set sail in an open stone coffin. A slow film of translucent water flowed beneath me, and the smiling faces of dead comrades were laid out in long rows at the bottom.

Watermark

Someone should make an inventory of the winds that constantly whistle over the water. They should list and describe all the river's different mists and fogs, for morning above the water is not the same as that above a freshly ploughed field. They should painstakingly record all the nuances of the river's dawn ordained by the accurate hand of a secret earthly chronometer and the inclination of the astral plane. What isn't put into words doesn't exist. To liken the crispness of the morning air I inhale through the window of my Grandmother's house to salutary mountain air would be to the detriment of the latter. This air has a special spice to it, a taste that can take you back to the age before the invention of the chariot. That aroma of freedom rising from the waterweed is erotic and intoxicating because it contains elixirs of eternal youth – an alchemy that cannot be fully described because it is never-ending like tufa, the stone that the tiny tufa-makers have built their stems and hearts into for tens of thousands of years.

The town can look like a freshwater Venice in the summertime with a mass of boats plying the river's by-channels and passing beneath bridges large and small. Adults and children sit and lie in those boats, chatting or silently gazing at their faces in the glass surface of the Una, until a roach or sneep jumps out of the water and returns with a big splash, leaving concentric circles on the surface that rush to be levelled out by touching the green banks. When you boat over the crystal-clear water and look down at the sandy bottom, you see an unreal sight, as if there was no water at all, or sand, or fish, and your boat is just gliding through time and space, detached from familiar earthly dimensions.

The human body in water hardly ever has the same martial aura as on land. Although your muscles glisten, wet with droplets, the cult of the body has only one purpose there: to strive against the river when swimming towards the foaming cascades so as to realize the full beauty of the water's power, and for a moment for it to become part of your muscles.

Someone should make a catalogue of all the cascades, rocky beds, deeps, shallows, greenholes and calm spots in the Una. They should give them names that will sound supernatural, but even that would not be enough for us to grasp the full sense of the Una's currents. As Joseph Brodsky writes in *Watermark*, 'There is something primordial about travelling on water, even for short distances.'

The River Bank in
Winter

It's winter and the water has risen as high as the earthen steps in the flat section of my Grandmother's courtyard. I dug those steps with a spade to make it easier to get to our small landing-pier because the bank is rather steep. Plum trees grow at the edge of the bank, which crumbles underfoot; the elder bush is self-seeded, and a little higher, up against the porch with the pump, there grows a solitary Scots pine, like in Catholic courtyards. Being so close to the house, it is always in the lee and gets little sun, so its needles are pale, in places almost yellowish, and it seems to be made of mist and the melancholy of the north.

Rickety fences now appear out of the water that has deposited yellow sand on the grass under the quince tree. The surface of the water is restless because the channel has become too narrow. Waves collide and spill into my Grandmother's courtyard. The water is so close that it beckons you to dip your hands into it.

Getting to the water here meant going all the way through the centre of town, running the gauntlet of people's goggling eyes. Eyes are just skilfully camouflaged in tense human bodies, pressed in like buttons, and those people hung out of shops, windows and cafés. I walked along, reeling off standard greetings to fellow townsfolk – 'Hello, Hi there, How are you?' – a small sacrifice compared to what came later. How could anyone like those gawkers? Blessed are the moles, for they're almost blind and don't peer anywhere. Moles are therefore much dearer to me than are most people.

Even before leaving my flat I would be seized by anxiety. I would quickly get dressed, annoyed that the winter was lasting so long, and start out on my pilgrimage. My ritual touching of the living thing that was the river, of watching the big bubbles that lifted grains of sand from the bottom, and that whole underwater turmoil of fluid tempests awakes in me only one desire: to become a fish with arms and legs.

Rain drips from the eaves of the house, and the cellar is flooded. When the water retreats, the cellar will be full of sand, branches, leaves and everything else that floats on the water's surface. The house is like a beacon, and through the living-room window full of light I can still see my Grandmother's face with its fine wrinkles; and I see the interior of the room that refused to obey the horizontal rule of the air bubble in the spirit level, instead standing at a slant and sinking in slow motion into the soft bank of the river.

Everything is different in the winter, including the behaviour of the water and the fish. The water is a translucent pale green and sometimes a transparent yellow like a balloon whose skin affords a hazy glimpse of a person, animal, object or event. The water is then in contingency mode, and the fish behave accordingly and are rarely seen. When you do catch a glimpse of them, they seem somehow pallid and tired from the cold that penetrates all the way to the riverbed. Deep below, the bullrushes have gradually lost their chlorophyll.

My grandmother's house is a gentle fortress with a chimney, moated by water. When there are floods, the water comes so close to the kitchen window that you can wash your hands in it. The hazelnut tree immediately below it serves as a mooring for boats. Further down is the sandy bank and several sewage pipes overgrown with moss. Above the house, an asphalt road leads to the river island, which has two football pitches. Above the road, houses stand packed together like grey crows in misty treetops. Here there are also concrete barriers on the rocky bank, whose purpose is long unknown and secret. Thorny brambles have now grown out of them and spilled out like a foaming wave. And moss has shown its splendour on their walls, as if the north resided right there in the concrete basins that once stored manure and other waste. Beside the basins the rock wall has flexed its muscles by rising out of the scant soil together with the robinias, showing the water level and the autograph of the river from times long before us.

My Grandmother's house is below the rock wall and the northern flats. Its courtyard runs parallel with it. A rose bush forms its centre, although it stands up against the fence of our upstream neighbour Ramo, who repairs pistols and rifles. The rose bush is the heart of the continental world the moment it flowers. The Una flows some 20m from it. My Grandmother is in the steep-floored kitchen on her prayer rug. When she prays, perfect silence fills the house. It's a house, whose every object smells of the river. When you lay your cheek on your pillow, you can hear the roar of the cascades and smell the sand, the fish and the freshwater mussels. I feel a premonition of my diving in the future, and that makes the palms of my hands sweat.

My Grandmother's house is in complete harmony with the water. It's a harmony, moreover, in which Arabic prayers mix with the pagan voices of piscine shamans. Grandmother is a frail pathfinder for her god, lost on the winter shore of this water-bound town. Her intimate god, Allah, is the only deity I ever believed to exist. I can see her at the threshold, drifting away from the bank as the house begins its journey, with grapevine sails and windows resembling human eyes. The opposite bank becomes ever further away and the Unadžik takes on the breadth of the sea. I let the house continue its voyage, although I am sorry because I know what it will turn into at its journey's end.

My Grandmother's house is in complete harmony with the water.

The Love

of Ruins

We pretended all the ruins didn't exist, but they were everywhere. You couldn't miss them. Our town had become a festival of ruins, and every day we charged foreigners for guided tours so they could photograph our burned houses and obliterated neighbourhoods. Our suffering was legendary, and we ourselves were exposed in more detail than in a weird porno film. Our town ranked third on the scale of the most devastated towns in Bosnia-Herzegovina. That wasn't exactly something to be proud of, but we had no choice other than to wallow in the mess we'd inherited.

We couldn't expect all those houses, factories and bridges to rise up again magically, out of water. The pockmarked streets couldn't grow a new skin. We passed between the ruins as if they were intimate monuments to our pre-war lives. Here and there, in Serbian houses, which we hadn't entered for years, some of us would find a photograph from our school days, from an excursion or of us hanging out together by the Una. Another guy saw the face of a former girlfriend, who had stayed on the enemy side; teenage love burned out faster than the cigarette of the soldier who was caught by mortar fire out in a meadow without any cover. Believe me, two or three puffs are enough to make you start smoking filter cigarettes. It's the fear that makes you smoke.

The iron bridge had been destroyed on *our* side of the river, and a load of pebbles was dumped there so we could at least somehow get across the Una, which flowed through the centre of town. Imagine a town with its Marshal Tito main street overgrown with weeds! Rumour-mongers say that the Chetniks kept pigs in the town's coffee house, but that's unrealistic because the centre of town was very close to the river and thus the front line, so pig-breeding would hardly have paid off. Less than thirty metres from there, the town's mosque had been blown up. Hideously deformedly by the explosion, its stones lay scattered all around. The minaret lay on top of the main heap of rubble like a telescope, through which believers were once able to summon and see the Absolute. The Orthodox Church, untouched, towered above the remains of the mosque, reflecting the balance of forces before we recaptured our town. I found a piece of blue and yellow stained glass from the mosque on the road there. I put it in my pocket.

We became very fond of the ruins. I went to the remains of my Grandmother's house in Pazardžik almost every day. Only the Unadžik was still largely unchanged. All the houses were gutted. The newer ones, made of brick, had the good fortune that at least their walls remained standing. I dug into the ruins of my Grandmother's house with my hands, assuming that that was where the living room had been, because one day before the war began I'd left a little gold chain in a box there, as well as precious photographs, letters and a .223 Remington hunting rifle with two handfuls of ammunition. All the rooms of the house were now one big heap of sand, tiles, mortar and stone. No one had yet developed a compass for coping in conditions such as these. My Grandmother's house had ceased to be three-dimensional, but the main stem of the grapevine survived the fire in the shelter of the new house we'd started building in Grandmother's garden.

Members of the Serb Democratic Party's paramilitary forces attacked the town from the direction of Lipik and the Grmeč foothills at 17:50 hours on 21th April 1992. Units of the Yugoslav People's Army were dug in above the town and were supposed to protect us from 'external enemies'. An alleged gun incident involving Muslim police reservists was given as the reason for the attack – the men were from the isolated village of Arapuša, which had a Bosnian Muslim majority and was surrounded by Serbian villages in the Grmeč foothills and outlying suburbs of Bosanska Krupa on the right bank of the Una. Innocent Serbian civilians were wounded in that imaginary incident, so a combined artillery and infantry attack was launched on the town. Only the blind would fail to notice the striking similarity with the simulated attack by SS units, disguised as Polish soldiers, on ethnic Germans near the city of Gleiwitz – a prelude to the destruction of Poland. Arapuša was later turned into a detention point, where civilians were confined in the houses before being transported to concentration camps or to unoccupied territory to be released.

I only began to notice the ruins when they no longer existed. While rubble towered at the sides of the streets like Cyclopean walls, the eye was used to the sight. The ruins gradually disappeared and new buildings, heavier and more ugly than the pre-war ones, sprouted from the debris of the former houses like plants from radioactive humus.

When I entered the town for the first time from the direction of the hospital, going down through the centre towards my block of flats, I felt suffocated by the bland realization that the town I knew had simply shrunk. My own body seemed huge and hard. I didn't see a single face, familiar or unfamiliar, at the windows of the houses. No one waved to me. The town was empty and almost dead, without a single resident. This is what the Earth would look like following a third world war and the twilight of civilization. Only an occasional curtain trembled briefly in a window before returning to its rigid state, like the eyelid of a person dying.

I arrived at my block of flats as ill prepared as Gulliver. This was like a dream I'd long known was coming, but now when I had to confront its realization I wasn't ready. The reality I saw was repulsively surrealistic. Let me be clear: I loved surrealism in literature and painting, but this was a film that made me feel sick. My titanic body versus the miniature town. I still hadn't noticed the ruins. The town's park may have gone to seed, but my building was the Gobi Desert with tiers and balconies, whose metal railings were being eaten by rust.

If I'd been in charge of the natural incidentals for this scene, I would have chosen a fine rain that slowly intensified. The soldier in the uniform of the Army of Bosnia-Herzegovina would keep standing, getting wetter and wetter in front of the entrance, above which a blue, bullet-riddled board read '89 Marshal Tito Street'. Then he would start vomiting.

I never joined the League of Communists of Yugoslavia. Once, in a Marxism class, I added my name to the list to become a member, but I changed my mind and crossed it out again. I didn't want to be in a party that anyone could join, without any check or test of their political convictions. There were many books that drew me away from blind faith in that system of ideas. And when I saw nationalists joining the League of Communists, or rather the pseudo-nationalists from my high school, my dreams of a cadre party fell apart. Only the naive could ask how it was possible for yesterday's communists to become ardent nationalists. The answer is clear: they were never communists.

Now my grey-green block of flats was in front of me, nothing else. A feral cat appeared on the balcony for a second or two and then quickly vanished into the living room. Now a holographic projection of the Romany Homer came out, moving his lips: 'Give me alms, good ladies, comrades, young folk... A small donation, may God giii-ve yoo-u heee-alth... May God proteee-ct your children...' His face looked like the hologram on a Schengen visa, a stylized circle truncated at the South and North Pole, from whose perforated bases rays with little concentric circles spread in all directions. In place of his eyes he had two golden lilies.

The rain would wash the vomit away downhill towards the place where the mosque and the Catholic church had been demolished but the Orthodox church remained whole; when we were bored at the guard post at Kareli's house, on our side of the Una, we took our rifles and used its copper cross for target practice, for a bit of fun. After all, we didn't have any larger-calibre weapons like a disintegration cannon to reduce the church to its atoms.

The colourful piece of stained glass has become my secret peacetime weapon. If I hold it up to my eyes I see what was, what is, and what will be: never again such beautiful ruins.

Blind

Spots

Although I knew the fakir could manipulate my ethical stance during hypnosis, I wasn't afraid at all, so I made myself go back to my blackest and most difficult memories – to what is inside each of us, though hardly anyone wants to admit their own wrongdoings. I am in my labyrinth and I'm not afraid. I have the strength to be ashamed for others. Shame is a murderous creature with the head of a bull – a bloodthirsty Minotaur that should be avoided at any price.

Half-dried blood from my unkempt mane gets between my fingers and under the nails. I touch my bloodshot eye and my mucous-covered tongue clenched between my teeth. The next-door neighbour lies dead in civilian clothing; no one wanted to see him being taken from his flat to the town rubbish dump. A long, echoing shot from a TT pistol blackened the sky with crows and the odd ponderous raven. I heard one man in a camouflage uniform say to the other: 'He got what was coming to him. Now he's free and can go wherever he wants.' They both laughed as they walked away through the rubbish. One of the uniformed men put his pistol back into the leather holster on his belt, then produced a whalebone comb from his breast pocket and tidied his hair. Swarms of crows and jackdaws cawed in flight as if they were casting spells at the earth. I was seized by superstition and became afraid of the birds. I felt the skin on my back crawl. So I quickly crammed the books into my rucksack, cursed the love of literature that made me root about in the town's rubbish for them, and entered the darkness of the forest, sticking to the safety of the path, which ferns stood over with their perverse smell.

There is only one way out of this labyrinth: through memory and speech. The brave learn to articulate their memory. Those who have sworn themselves to silence find a different refuge from the shadows of horrible events – 'six feet under'. Gargano is the kind of man who will take his secret with him to the grave.

How distant we were from the crimes that took place before our eyes. Sometimes we would talk about the soldiers of the 'Vitezovi' battalion (The Knights), who beheaded captive Serbs on the battlefield. Some saw that as reason to admire the military effectiveness of those soldiers and the bravery required to cut a person's throat and chop off their head, thus raising the notional number of enemy dead. Enthusiasts like that, in cushy dens far behind the lines, thought wartime reality was similar to the Counter-Strike video game, while the more innocent would feel queasy or even sick at the images of decapitation. We rarely talked about such 'events', which weren't referred to by anyone as war crimes back then. The struggle for sheer survival could justify all kinds of raids and actions, especially when you're trapped in an enclave – a concentration camp in the open – with three enemy armies fighting against you: the Bosnian Serbs, the Serbs from the Knin area in Croatia, and Abdić's Autonomists. There's no room here for humanism and the Renaissance, we thought at the time, and I don't remember anyone ever using the expression 'war crimes', which I first heard on CNN in connection with the Omarska and Keraterm concentration camps, and afterwards in the stories whispered around after the fall of Srebrenica. The Information and Morale Section of our army didn't tell us the real truth about Srebrenica. The 'moralists', as usual, read us the latest censored news from the combat zones in eastern Bosnia. Their reports gave some casualty figures, but they were nowhere near the real figure of eight thousand men taken prisoner and then killed. They listed in detail the number of enemy tanks, other vehicles, light infantry weapons and the amount of ammunition captured when our fighters broke out of the Srebrenica and Žepa enclaves and headed for unoccupied territory near Tuzla, which was supposed to be a consolation. The fall of Srebrenica was presented more as a harsh military defeat, less as a war crime (or not at all), although you could sense the bitterness in the words and between the lines. I wouldn't find out the real truth until the very end of the war when military secrets became senseless, but even then I was far from able to realize the scale of the Srebrenica tragedy, which the International Criminal Tribunal in The Hague would later declare to be genocide. I went on with my own life. My view was narrowed and I couldn't see the whole fresco, only its parts.

We heard stories about the torture of Autonomists, both the notorious and those ostensible ones, and of the occasional Serb from Cazin (of the two or three who lived in the town) under accusation of being spies, in moments when the situation on the ground facing the Autonomists was difficult and we were on the verge of collapse. Rumours had it that the torture was carried out by local or 'imported' criminals in the service of the civilian police. They were said to give electric shocks to the testicles of the prisoners or make them eat salt, after which they were given gallons of water to drink under threat of death. But even these stories didn't particularly disgust us because we considered the Autonomists (particularly them) and the Chetniks to be organic enemies, who were to be shown no mercy in hand-to-hand combat; or maybe we were just on the worst of battlefields, where all your thoughts are subordinate to auto-suggestion: 'I'm gonna get through this, I'm gonna get through this...'

There was also talk of captured Serbs from our local battlefield of Ćojluk having been beaten to death with spades and steel cables from downed power lines. I was able to assemble that image, but it jarred in my mind because I couldn't conceive of prisoners being tormented when they were unarmed and helpless in a cellar far behind our lines – when they were stripped of all features of the 'sinister enemy'. Torture was the job of the military police, and they beat the Chetniks so they wouldn't have to go to the front line themselves. Some of the torturers did it to avenge a dead brother, daughter or son. But I didn't know anyone like that.

I lie: I knew an older man who saw his dead son in every prisoner and therefore proceeded to thrash them. With every blow he withered away a bit more, dwindling as he rushed to meet his son.

The old man's strength was superhuman. He didn't know how else to kill his pain, so death was the only drug for him. Something was eating away at him inside at a galloping pace, and shortly before he died he had shrunk from a colossus to the size of a spindly schoolboy. The prisoners he beat black and blue are also dead. The circle of their life is closed. All of them sit together in a circle in the Elysian Fields of their home with their legs folded Indian-style – borderland Cossacks smoking home-grown tobacco and looking down into the sky; Zaporozhians, whose sole religion was meat and blood. And rakia, of course, ubiquitous and indispensable. When they laugh, the sun shines and the rain falls.

During my time at an army supply base, one fellow-soldier showed me a hangar where captured Serbs from Ćojluk were tortured and killed, and buried nearby, from where they would later be exhumed and transported to prisoner exchanges, or rather corpse exchanges. I don't remember there ever being any exchanges of living prisoners in our combat zone.

I slept several nights near that hangar for torturing and killing. We were close to a mountain with a relay station on top, so we had the good fortune of being able to pick up Croatian state television. Early in the evenings we would watch the quiz show *Numbers and Letters*. The host waved his arms theatrically and the audience clapped when they were supposed to. Every time one of the quiz participants turned the wheel of fortune, a soldier up on the bunk bed would pronounce, 'The wheel of fortune spins: someone loses, someone wins', and then he started to whistle a jumbled melody made up on the spur of the moment. This in no way disturbed the host with his energetic arms and well-fitting suit, the quiet middle-aged audience and the wheel of fortune he turned every Thursday, bringing contentment to anonymous elder folk in the Croatian provinces. The peace he made to radiate from those faces was shocking for me: I saw only the bovine satisfaction that comes with rumination – a dullness bordering on the brilliant.

Before the war, that hangar had been used for raising and fattening cattle. It made me feel sick, and neither water nor the passage of years could wash the blood from that place. I thought

about it having been the 'duty' of those people to torture and to execute, but that thought never lasted long because the revulsion I felt became a creeping madness; until turning off my brain became the best solution.

I never set foot inside that hangar – I detoured it unconsciously, and sometimes semi-consciously. For me, it was a place tainted with the death of my enemies, and a particle of my own death could potentially be there too, a tiny embryo that I feared. A few hundred metres from there was the battlefield of Ćojluk, where my death languished and waited for me in the bare hills. I would have most liked to run away, but I was ashamed. Death is everywhere and doesn't takes sides, it doesn't care about ethnicity and isn't politically correct. It leaves a trail of blood and the stench of bodies and fear behind it. Those are its subjects, inanimate workers who pour molten lead into your marrow, taking your breath away and turning your legs to tree trunks fused with the centre of the Earth, so there is no way of fleeing – as if in a haunting dream. The hangar was a forbidden space and I gave it wide berth.

Meanwhile the audience in *Numbers and Letters* applauded frenetically, and I felt like plunging into the cathode tube, ripping out the wheel of fortune and using it as a rudder, a machine-gun or a shuriken to chop off all their heads. Blood glistened under the doors of the hangar like fruit syrup on a cake. Exhaled air turned to little clouds of steam. I lit a cigarette, collected my thoughts, and breathed in the sharp mountain air. Wild dogs howled over at Gomila, while a tubercular moon sailed the sky above Ćojluk. I was full of life, and no horror could spoil the pleasure of that feeling for me.

During our great offensive, we came across a woman in a largely Serbian village. She didn't want to flee with the other residents and had decided to stay at home. The houses at the beginning of the wealthy, bucolic village had been meticulously torched because they had belonged to Muslims. The style of arson showed the thoroughness of the local 'cleansers' in charge of the purity of God's chosen Serbian people. There was no time for me to think what had become of the former residents.

The woman was middle-aged and healthily stout, with rosy cheeks like two apples beneath her bound headscarf. She sat at the table in her courtyard as if nothing was happening. The horror had completely calmed her. We ran into her by coincidence because the operation involved entering the village from several directions, so there was the usual traffic jam and confusion when units of different brigades came together.

I heard her speaking to some of the soldiers milling around nearby: 'Are you Serbs too? You are, I know it. You just don't want to say you're Serbs...', which irritated our Bosnian soldiers.

I'm not sure if I heard the burst of machine-gun fire while I was still in her field of vision or when I'd gone around behind the barn, hurrying to accomplish our objective of taking the high ground. I don't remember – I may even have seen her collapse and convulsively clutch at the waxed tablecloth, pulling the stainless-steel tray with the coffee service down onto the bright green grass covered with morning dew and knocking over the table, but afterwards my mind refused to preserve that vision of the crime. Your thoughts are racing at a hundred miles per hour at moments like that, and everything beyond your immediate goal flashes by in that waking nightmare.

After that machine-gun burst, we continued on towards our hill through the descending September darkness. As we were passing the Orthodox church, we heard the firing of a Wasp rocket launcher and an explosion. The commander of a sabotage unit appeared and told me and my men to take cover because there was Chetnik shelling, although it was clear that they themselves were trying to demolish the church with Wasps. When we finally reached the hilltop without being ambushed, we spread out along the ridge and dug in well. No enemies attacked us because they were seriously out of it. We stayed in the area for ten days. The houses had electricity, and we watched Croatian state television as if hypnotized. In terms of ammunition, weapons, food and cigarettes, those were the golden days of the war, and its last. We withdrew without a fight in pitch-black night by order of senior command. I remember the code 801 they sent to my Motorola, which meant immediate withdrawal. The village vanished behind us in the darkness. Succulent bell peppers hung ripe in its gardens and surrounding fields, flourished by the fertile, sandy soil. Their colour was poignantly reminiscent of the cheeks of the peasant woman seconds before she was shot.

Elegy for a
Toshiba

My imaginary Alexandrian library, the one that should consist of small items, innocuous daily rituals and fragments of memory, also contains an old Toshiba cassette recorder. I bought it at a bookshop sometime in the early 1980s, and that cassette recorder with two heads was the first model whose buttons were at the bottom, immediately under the flap for the cassettes. It was light and well made, neither too tall nor too bulky, and of black plastic. It had a radio scale, whose gleam at night could whisk me away to distant places like Riga or Vilnius, cities whose location I didn't know for sure at the time. Their names seemed as if they came from another planet, and the Baltic and non-Slavic parts of the USSR were just that, with the exception of the Lithuanian basketball players in the Soviet team. The cassette recorder aged at the same pace as other devices, as design progressed and ever faster and crazier new functions evolved. Capitalism, still remote and beyond the Berlin Wall, worked wonders that we would see in delayed action, when it had already lost emotional value for us. We would be lost in the remnants of our own and others' lives, in our attempts to rebuild them and rediscover wholeness and simple happiness. The 1990s therefore have power over us like totalitarian memory. I am one, but there are thousands of us – the unbreakable, broken ones.

The film *Blade Runner* shows massive advertising boards for the TDK Corporation on top of the buildings in a futuristic city constantly lashed with rain. I'll always remember that brand for its 60 and 90-minute cassettes. There is sure to be a hidden planet somewhere, a world for lost things and objects that have gone out of fashion, their ads pulsating with the neon radiance of non-ephemerality. I now realize that this cassette recorder will be an exhibit high up on the scale of importance in my imaginary Alexandrian library. I've always been too quick to renounce material objects, and if I'd known what was about to happen I would have carried it with me through water, fire and mud. But no, I left it in Zagreb on the 15th April 1992 and returned to my country, already in the grips of war.

Eastern Bosnia was attacked by units of the Yugoslav People's Army together with numerous, well-armed bands of criminals from Serbia under the guise of countering 'Muslim extremism' ('the Green Berets') and fighting to preserve Yugoslavia. I saw with my own eyes the refugees from Zvornik standing with plastic bags and bundles in the car park of Zagreb's mosque. Those were people of flesh and blood, the first Bosnian refugees sent off into the world like tracer bullets in the night sky, scattered in all directions. We'd gone to the mosque to convince ourselves of what we heard from Radio Sarajevo's reporters on the ground. The radio journalist from the east-Bosnian town of Foča didn't know who was shooting at whom there. Confusion was rife. For the civilians floating down the rivers Drina and Ćehotina, the war was unmistakably over because they were dead. Rallies for peace and the preservation of Yugoslavia had been held in Sarajevo several days earlier. Feeble-minded miners and workers, the urban underclass, marched with Yugoslav flags and socialist songs on their lips until Chetnik snipers ensconced in the Holiday Inn made them scatter. I was twenty-five years old and didn't feel any sympathy for them. Whoever wanted to die like an idiot had my full support.

Out on a battlefield in the late autumn of 1994, when the leaves bled in pastel colours along with the men, I rescued a Sanyo cassette recorder from a house that was about to burn down to the foundations – fire is the *good* spirit of our time. The cassette recorder would last me all of fourteen years.

The Zlovrh battlefield was one of mud and rain, rain and mud, like the Russian front in late autumn before the snow, ice and biting cold set in. Everything sinks into the ground, plants droop and die, and the ash-grey mire devours all hope that the sun will ever shine

again. Our front was worse than the Russian front in books because we had no broad steppes to retreat across; but there was that front inside us. When I first think of it I feel a chill in my bones, but later it becomes a pleasant source of warmth – a stove I don't invoke, yet it warms me. Then Rutger Hauer turns up in a long leather coat, as the rain pours at the front line, and, making his way through thorny bushes with his bare hands, constantly repeats to us: 'This isn't time to die. This isn't time to die...'

Even after I stopped using it, long after the war, it continued to stand among the functional objects around me as a protective relic of at least some kind of past – my past. Its plastic jacket had pretty much melted on one side in the heat of the fire. That wartime scar meant that it finally ended up in a rubbish skip on the steep side of town when I moved house.

During my fragmentary dream I saw the Toshiba cassette recorder before me. It lay smashed open on the table, with its wires only just holding it together. Its display gave off a faint blue gleam, and inside its works were almost untouched, with rows of distinctive yellow diodes that looked like a transformer station. Solitary monuments of an old technology like ghost towns from the Wild West – that's what its insides looked like. Its exterior was broken, but it still worked. Weren't we all like that straight after the war? Unaware of how we were damaged by omnipresent corrosion, but full of the mad adrenalin of survivors.

The cassette recorder and many other lost things, especially those that aren't material – lost emotions and memories of the shadow of some toy in the distant twilight ten thousand nights ago – are what impelled me to build my Alexandrian library. That is the duty of an archivist of melancholy. When I put a new item in the library it automatically closes. My past fills up and the emptiness of the world becomes less. The library mysteriously fades from view, as befits it, and I can then be a more or less happy archivist of my past.

Centaur

In a completely different dream, thick warm snow was falling. My sister and I were walking through a town. It was quiet and easily recognizable as our town, and yet a little different or unusual, as things often are in dreams. We stood in the central square, which must have had some kind of under-floor heating because the snowflakes melted as soon as they touched its stone blocks, which were wonderfully coloured. The square was a brilliant, intricate mosaic with lamp-posts and old-fashioned benches around the edges. I marvelled at the colours of the large slabs: they were rich and beautiful, and the smooth stonework even felt like it was living matter that could soak up moisture like a sponge if you wanted it to. A gaily-coloured tram suddenly passed down the main street, which ran down one side of the square, merrily ringing its bell through the downy puffs of snow.

We talked about how strange it was that we hadn't noticed the beauty of our town before, with the novelties of the colourful square and the trams, but we weren't overly astonished – we accepted the town as it had become. We stayed on at the square. My sister was wearing a chequered coat of warm winter fabric; I couldn't see myself well because I was absorbing all the colours, the snow and the warmth, despite it being a freezing day. A general feeling of warmth and comfort pervaded my body. In my dream I was completely aware of it being a dream, but that in no way lessened its charm for me. Perhaps I wandered off for a second or two and forgot that I was dreaming. Then I went with the flow of the dream to the place where our town was doubly beautiful. It was reminiscent of the staid little town in peacetime, in the late 1970s or early 1980s, but it also had something of a future that might one day come.

Without smokestacks the sky would be free for birds, pagan gods and aeroplanes. In the Old Town, instead of heavy guns and howitzers from the Second World War, there would be models of Alice in Wonderland, Godzilla, King Kong, Flipper and other imaginary heroes on show. The Una would perhaps be navigable for one part of the year (for the rest it would be the same, transparent and green) and tugboats – vessels full of melancholy – would glide down it lazily. This would open the possibility of a poem of boats, water and long journeys, further spreading the world of the river in the spirit of mariners' cosmopolitanism.

Now I'm waiting for snow like that to fall so I can see my town as a perfect mélange of Sarajevo, Zagreb and a faraway Levantine city I've never been to, except in my dreams. The first snowflakes descend from the clouds and I close my eyes.

When you're in search of the missing, you become a chronicler of dreams. I therefore had to induce myself to dream, and in the dream to devise everything that didn't exist in reality so as better to describe it in a waking state. Even when my dreams were to do with projections of the future, at an even deeper level I dreamed of the past. I had no choice and searched for inspiration wherever I could.

Smith the Redeemer,
AKA the Conductor of Clouds

I saw the impact-action rifle grenade come down three metres in front of us with my own eyes. It had plastic stabilizer fins at the tail, and the body of the grenade looked like some kind of green, army grayling, 20 cm long, and its diameter was the same along its whole length. For a moment it seemed to hang in the air, and the leaves stopped falling from the trees, or stopped in the air, while we were off the ground, bounding like springboks and trying to get as far away as possible. We were caught in a vacuum beneath the forest canopy in October when trees change colour like the face of a mortally ill person, who, tired of the shell of their body, waits for it to expire. And so the leaves waited for the performance to end and the light to be extinguished by the hand of someone or something greater than ourselves, on the peak of that forested hill where we had the shit beaten out of us, after which nothing would ever be the same any more, at least in terms of the scars on body and mind. And at one moment we dropped to the ground, the grenade burst, and everything was blown to smithereens. The Earth turned upside down, the arthritic roots of the trees spread from my eyes, the men in front of us were lying on the ground, and the sky below them grimaced. Then I heard a scarcely audible sound above my head and a breath of air that raised the hair on my head; everything went black and soil came raining down. I hadn't been hit by a single piece of shrapnel, but the fellow next to me was deader than JFK. A long, triangular shadow grew, and I caught a glimpse of him in his raincoat pierced by shell fragments as he soared into the forest and ripped through the canopies of the trees sopping wet from three days of rain. Stronger and more real than Superman, Batman and Spiderman put together, he didn't care if anyone else saw him apart from me as he pushed through the canopies of the trees with his

175

gory shrapnel-hands, and the rainwater showered us down on the ground. It fell on the dead soldier and his bearded face, where death took root in a millisecond, making blood from his chest gush out over the yellow clay of the forest track. A stratus cloud settled over the ground and concealed us from enemy eyes.

I knew that was Smith the Redeemer, who had helped me countless times during the war and thanks to whom I can now talk about all this with a cool head and write with a steady hand. It was to him that I owed my bravery and wartime exploits, as a result of which I received several bonuses. But still I wasn't awarded the ultimate medal, the Bosnian Golden Lily, because the brigade commander hated my guts and I didn't know how to lick his arse.

Whenever fear took hold – that utter fear that seizes even the nitrogen molecules in the air, he would appear and free me of the fear of death, and then I would be as light as a hummingbird and fast as a virus. That's why I decided to look for him at the return address on the letter I received after the war, signed with his name. I found the apartment in 5 Emily Dickinson Street on the third floor of a grey building that looked like a sick pigeon, as Fernand Léger would have imagined it. It was a flat worthy of the prophet of a non-existent religion, which he was in his own right, though no one had yet raised kitsch statues to him like the ones in Catholic churches that made me feel nauseous as a small boy, in fear of the death that the cold interior smelled of. The relics of his bones weren't encased in gold and silver like reliquaries. Whenever I see a pendant with a hair of a saint or some other reliquary, I realize with sadness how little of God is left on Earth. How primitive people are if they believe that a forearm with a hand cast in gold, with unnaturally slender fingers and golden nails, can possess the supernatural power to do anything other than stand around in a glass case with less kinetic energy than the cheapest jelly vibrator made in China.

Everywhere the algebra of chaos: inside out clothes, leaves of paper and littered objects. I entered the flat, which had been abandoned in a great hurry. The walls of Smith's study were covered with sketches of atmospheric grey. Sketches of ten types of clouds: the delicate wisps of cirri; cirrocumuli like small sheep; veil-like cirrostratus; altocumuli (white or grey rags, rolls and rounded heaps); altostrati (bluish cloud cover); nimbostrati that bring rain, snow and sleet, stratocumuli (whitish rags with dark parts); strati that bring drizzle and granular snow; cumuli (mounds, domes and towers); and cumulonimbi (huge mountains and towers) – the most noteworthy clouds in the sky, whose energy is equal to that of several atomic bombs, and all their types and variations. These brief descriptions of clouds were spelled out in his handwriting.

The clouds' time of formation and duration was carefully noted on a two-metre-wide roll of paper pasted from ceiling to floor along the length of the wall. He didn't have a bedroom for the simple reason that he never slept. A being of his rank had no need for sleep – that is for us mortals. The wind tried in vain to drive the curtains into the room, banging the wooden venetian blinds against the façade and back towards the window. The pungent aroma of surgical spirit still hung in his study, while the floor of the bathroom-toilet was covered by a heap of dried-up faeces that had no smell at all. It had gone hard, was six feet high, and had obviously been shaped into a symmetrical hill of excrement, which stretched from where the toilet bowl should have been to the bath. There were wads of cotton wool soaked in alcohol on the floor, which suggested he had cleaned his body with them because the shower mixer had been ripped out and stopped up with plaster. That was all that remained of Smith the Redeemer: clouds and shit. No messages on the fridge door under a magnetic holder. In the fridge I saw a jar with a frozen yellow Una maggot inside. I sat down on the couch, reached out for the pile of books on the floor, blew the dust off the title-page and started reading *The Catcher in the Rye*. I expected the end of the world or something similar. The regular afternoon delirium gripped people in their lower-middle-class flats, where the television represents the door to perception, to both heaven and hell. But everyone kept pretending they were normal. No one tore open the window and screamed at the top of their voice. The wind dropped away, and for a few seconds absolute silence reigned. The first drops were as silent as a cat's footfall. The rain started its white back-jets, ever stronger and faster. In the flat across from

Smith's an elderly man masturbated while looking at photos of scantily clad teenage girls on Facebook, who revealed to the whole world how enamoured they were in their own bodies. There was time for sleeping, for alcohol, and for popping the amazing two-coloured pills that could launch me into the maw of the astral lizard. Smith the Redeemer had betrayed me again like he did the time I chased him over the river islands and across the Una. I fell asleep on a couch in a flat in a part of Sarajevo I'd never been to before. I dreamed I was writing this book and that I'd never finish it.

The House on
Two Waters

The house by the Una had its rises and falls. It burned down the first time in 1942 during the Allied bombing of the town, and only a heap of ash was left. The household members gathered around it as if it were the grave mound of a dearly departed relative. In the time that followed, the wind blew the ash away over the river and a new house was built of tufa and Una sand, but with timber for the stairs, reeds for the panelling and oaken beams for the diagonal supports of the walls. That was the house I remember, and it would meet with the same fate, except that it was destroyed in a different way – by a dirty, uncouth hand in 1992 that held a cigarette lighter to a sheet of paper that fell in slow motion on to a petrol-doused carpet, which would sweep the house away into the sky. With the words 'you'll rise to the sky in smoke' in his poem 'Death Fugue', Paul Celan unknowingly wrote an epitaph for my Grandmother's house.

Those were its earthly downfalls, but the inner world is quite different, and here the house continues its existence. Its residents are still living inside, in that airy space. In the summer, the wonderful aroma of roasted coffee rises from the roasting drum on the porch formed by the roof, which slants steeply down to the part of the courtyard facing the river. The grapevine extends its tendrils across the posts of the porch and the water gurgles from the metal pump, and before it pours into the concrete trough it murmurs in strange voices like a creature freed from heavy fetters in the blackest depths of the earth that finally breaks out into the light of day. My Grandmother, her face framed in a headscarf of soft colours, waters the rose bush in the garden, which sprouted out of the rich, sandy soil you can find only on the banks of the Una.

The smell of its petals is intoxicating, and Grandmother will make them into a sweet, pale-red cordial in two-litre jars. The petals will rest on the surface for a while and then start sinking towards the placid, sugary bed. Where the garden ends and the courtyard begins, wild chamomile and plantago grow. There is a bench with a table beneath the quince tree, and just three steps further is our greenhole and the small landing-pier. The boats there are heavy and their ribs – planks bent to the shape of angular horseshoes – are damp from constantly being in the water. The boats are used for extracting sand and going fishing. Whoever has a boat also has a pier, and every pier is named after the owner of the boat, just like greenholes bear the surname of the family that lives closest.

My Grandmother's second house, the one I remember, had been sinking into the bank, facing the river, for years. The floor in the kitchen was already steep as if the house was in the process of sliding into the water. Grandmother didn't like this, and she always dreamed of a firm, reliable stone embankment to stop what was impossible to stop: the unity of the river and time, like in Heraclitus' metaphor.

On the bank below the house there was a hazelnut tree, skimpy but spry, and I would sometimes watch the kingfisher sitting in it with the celestial colours on its neck feathers and its black, silent beak pointing towards the water, as if it was aiming at a fish swimming carelessly close to the surface. In late autumn, the kingfisher would sit there on a bare branch for hours, without any catch, until the rain came. It destroyed the clarity of the river, making it a terrible monster of incomprehensible tongue and broad, murky musculature that instilled fear and apprehension. When the kingfisher darts towards the water it becomes an awl that stabs the water with a gentle plop and comes up with a fish in its bill, which it takes to a willow branch. Drops of water would cling to its oiled plumage, and their shine would intensify the bright, paradisiacal colours on its neck and chest. In the summer, the kingfisher would be invisible in the leaves of alders, willows or aspens, which would turn the white undersides of their leaves in gusts of wind that signalled rain and storm.

It's hard to describe the house in winter, coated in snow and with icicles hanging precipitously from the edge of the roof. The fire in the sheet-metal stove reigned then, and often some orange peel or the fragrant piece of elecampane root from my Grandmother's china closet lay on top of it quietly drying. Whoever liked watching the water also enjoyed the fire. Tiny tongues of flame licked through the little door of the stove, which was a space catapult that would launch us into unknown, balmy landscapes without wet snow and the raging Una. My Grandmother's prayer rug was a source of warmth – a treated sheepskin with white locks, on which she prayed to her god five times every day. The china closet displayed glass dishes, old documents with the seal of the Kingdom of Serbs, Croats and Slovenes, golden jewellery and bottles of rakia with medicinal herbs for making compresses. None of those things cared much for human perceptions of time. There was also a locked drawer that I only managed to peek into sometimes when Grandmother took out her golden ring with the opal, which changed its hues before my eyes when I turned it towards the light fixture with its hidden light bulb.

Winter by the river wasn't exactly fun. The house was a sarcophagus that sealed us in until the coming of spring and divine summer, unless Uncle Šeta performed a trick for us like making a coin disappear from the palm of his hand or swallowing a chain – magic he learned during his time in the Yugoslav navy.

My Grandmother's house stood on two waters, at the boundary of two worlds, and leaned of its own accord towards the River Una, the other indescribable river, into which it would finally sink one day. Then I would be able to see it as part of a sunken city full of nymphs and water sprites, and I would recognize the contours of my face in the water's depths.

The Una will keep flowing after I finish my story.

I returned to this real river and mixed with its colour and strength, but the sun was already tracing willow veins onto the smooth surface of the water. The radio broadcast of a Sunday football match came from behind the curtains of a house's open window. Laundry on the line, as dry as gunpowder, danced in the west wind. Everything was possible, near and touchable. Over near where the river takes a turn past the abandoned abattoir in the cascades full of air bubbles, I see a thirteen-year-old boy with a fishing rod in his hand, making his way through the mint and long grass by the riverside, and then disappearing in its wild waves.

The First Words

of the Book

Let us imagine it's raining outside, simply because the watery mood is good for writing. I think of mushrooms springing out of the moist soil right now: first the little caps emerge, then the upright bodies. A man walks through the forest and his feet sink into the damp leaves underlaid with soft humus. He's a magician who can turn a metal bar into a wisp of smoke when the roof of the factory he's set fire to at the edge of town melts. (There are always two magicians, black and white; the white magician would turn a metal bar in the hands of a killer into a slimy snake.) The black magician walks through the forest, a wide-brimmed hat on his head. His face is hidden. His trousers are wet to the knees from the forest undergrowth. I stop the rain. I delete the magician because I don't like black. I put sea horses above the forest, and they drift and make faint, high-pitched noises as they ride on columns of air bubbles. But how can sea horses be flying above a continental forest of hornbeams and beeches? The mushrooms return to the earth. The rain retires to the clouds. But a different, terrible rain now pours into all my wounds. Various creatures and stories strive to get out of me, fleeing before the great flood that's coming. I ought to start saving what can be saved. Words, figurines of speech, sketches, and creatures like the mad Gargano and various objects ought to be put on board a sturdy ship.

I hastily opened a file at the computer and started brainstorming names for the book, all of them in two parts:

A nature novel (Life with an IOU)

Night time notes (The AK-47 and its meteors)

Quiet flows the Una (A Balkan requiem)

A book of nature (A nocturne for Yugoslavia)

A brief glossary of melancholy (I broke down into atoms)

A brief glossary of sadness (The book of mist)

A brief glossary of everything (An epitaph for ants and lizards)
A brief glossary of the world that disappeared in the whistle of the mist's steam engine
A brief glossary of the world that disappeared in the whistle of the rainbow's blackbird
A brief glossary of the aquatic world (Ethereal soldiers)
A brief glossary of the Una (The green book).

I had to start somewhere, and the titles seemed like a good beginning. When I'd chosen the name for that sturdy boat I embarked all my inhabitants and set off downstream towards the sea in a grand and glorious adventure of writing. And that vessel is called Quiet Flows the Una.

I'm not sure what's become of all the other names and whether I've managed to incorporate some of them into the book, at least superficially. Whenever I tried to flee from myself:

to the safety of the greenery,

to the calm of a greenhole,

to Manaus, in the steamy rainforests, where a cricket counts the seconds of summer in the muggy night;

something would always bring me back.

Whether the public TV Teledex was fraught with:

the excavation of mass graves,

reports from the trials of war criminals,

world news about volcanoes erupting,

earthquakes,

civil aviation catastrophes,

outbreaks of mysterious viruses and the threat of nuclear war.

All these things drove me from my original intention of saying I'm sick of myself and fed up with writing about the war and its consequences, and that I want to flee to the idyllic world of my childhood by the River Una. But it shouldn't be a classical book about growing up (I'm opposed to growing up) because I was overloaded with people and tired of the inane clutter of their lives. I wanted there to be as few people as possible in the book. Of course, I didn't succeed in my intention of writing a calm book about water, plants and animals because my desire was insincere and resulted from the pressure of my environment to adopt pseudo-narratives. In the end, I've resigned myself to the journey, guided by instinct, that most reliable of compasses, towards uncharted land. Of all the uncertainties I have to live with, the only thing I am certain about is my reason for writing this book.

Objects couldn't last. They would get lost without a trace, or they would break and fall to shreds, little pieces and dust. I wanted things to last. I always wanted to have one or more things that would go through time together with me. I needed that kind of inanimate travelling companion who would be completely subject to my will. I wasn't a dictator; it was clearly the wish to have something I could always rely on. I imagined things of the hardest metal, for example a titanium watch that would be indestructible like Stalingrad. That watch would last without a single scratch. I hated to think of the moment when my object would suffer some mechanical damage; then it would be sullied for me, less valuable; I would lose faith in its healing powers, and that would be the end of our time together. But Titan and I would be inseparable. It would never leave my wrist. Its luminous pointers were hands of light, and they would show me the way when darkness fell and shadowy outlines were the only visual cues in the material world.

Titan's hand points to the cascade
Where Šeta comes up to the surface with a fish on his harpoon
Water droplets shine on the grayling's fin
The nuances of summer explode in the fish's eye.

There had to be something that would withstand the erosion of time, something sturdier than my life and my body. Clothing was unreliable because it wore out so quickly. It grew thin like snow before the gusts of the south wind. It became threadbare beneath my clammy hands, and from rain, sun and washing machine. I soon discarded my toys. There was no point in developing an intimate bond with them because they're only made to last for one phase of life, and when you outgrow them they're simply pitiable. Why should I collect objects that will provoke pity in me? Nostalgia is a fine thing, but I needed something more: an object that would show no signs of wear and tear – a diamond pocketbook full of an alchemist's notes for saving the Earth and for the advancement of humankind – the ultimate object, into which I could integrate my subtlest feelings, and in which I would build a shrine to my solitude. Being alone and enjoying solitude is the peak of intimacy with the world that surrounds me. But objects, chattels, jewellery and watches couldn't last. Everything of firm material was prone to destruction or disappearance, so what could I then rely on? I raised defensive walls of strong, futile objects in vain. I secluded myself among books and other beloved fetishes, and dust collected on them to warn me of the fragility of matter. As soon as you make a world, a house or a hut of sticks, it is doomed to failure; it was already doomed back when it was a black and white sketch in your head. That's why I began to believe in words. They cannot be destroyed. If you erase them, they come back. Words float in front of your eyes and won't retreat from the front line. If you set fire to them, they will burn with even greater ardour in your memory, and no memory-wipers like alcohol or narcotics will get rid of them. Words are above destruction. If you erase them, they're right back on the tip of your tongue again. That's why I started describing just things that were important to me, like a maniac:

'The mounted tusks of a prize wild boar killed in the same year as I was born used to hang just inside the front door of the flat on the narrow strip of wall immediately on the right, above the light switch. When you pass the trophy, the living-room door is directly to the right, and the hallway to my bedroom goes off parallel with the trophy. To the left of the bedroom is a narrow kitchen with its window looking out on to terraced gardens full of lush green plants. If you continue straight on from the front door, that's the way to the bathroom and the toilet with cold, little white tiles. My things are in particular places in my bedroom: the herbarium full of pressed leaves and a mass of flowers, my letters, the handwritten results of the 1982 Football World Cup in Spain, and erotic magazines are all stacked

in the compartments of a massive, X-shaped table with a stand in the middle. The table is upside down so as to take up less space and leans against the wall on one arm immediately behind the room's glass door. The moment I sit down in the lounge and start watching Hollywood faces smile with their gleaming white teeth on the screen, I'm not aware that they're actually long dead. It would take a whole book for me to describe just that lounge. An army of a hundred thousand words wouldn't be enough to seize that space and jam it between the covers of a book. Now you know your way about my flat and can be part in its reconstituted three-dimensionality.'

I hoped this act of description would make my objects firm and indestructible in the world that surrounded me like an endless dark forest. Everything that was gone forever could be rebuilt with words, I thought. I paid homage to my dead comrades and thus reached an understanding with that part of my bereavement. But the loss of the pre-war world of emotions and the palpable objects that comprised it – living rooms (the universe of the intimate), books (time machines) and photographs (time conserved in crystal) – was manifested for me as extreme pain.

Writing would allow me to make myself a crutch, a substitute world. They say books last longer than people, and I agree, but an ordinary copper hairpin is more durable than whole generations of people. As confounding as that is, I decided I would write down for myself everything that I dreamed and told the fakir when I came out of hypnosis. I would use autohypnosis to make the memory of the séance come back and then, in a waking state, speak everything into a tape recorder. Later I would put my fears into a book and thus incorporate myself into something that would last, without any idea what purpose it would have for others. When I did that, I realized how far I'd strayed from my initial intention of linking up with my past, of feeling it with my hands as one would embrace the face of a beloved person, tenderly and with a tremble. I registered the changes I experienced during this journey in painstaking detail, not wanting to let anything go, not even those images of crimes I would prefer to bury at the remotest point of the Milky Way; no, I recorded them too. Every tiny detail I saw in my memory or reimagined in a random flashback can be made into a colour in life's fresco. The pine needles and buds of the white pine behind my Grandmother's house could take on colour. After the war we cut down that tree, as inexplicable as it is to me now, in the hope of starting back from square one, unaware that there is no 'square one'. We stood forlornly at the smoking ruins of our former homes, in a state of enduring shock and accustomed to the brutality of what we saw; we were those shards from Guernica, living beings that walked the ruins, devoted to the automatisms of clearing away rubble and reordering the blighted town. That was the best we could do in our situation. (My Grandmother's house had been reduced to a mound of rubbish and only a pipe jutted up where the kitchen sink used to be, with a trickle of water flowing from it for months after the war.)

When I touched sacred objects from my past and finally became whole, I was disturbed once more to realize that the war and its temporal-spatial discontinuity weren't the only cause of my trauma. It was also caused by the tiny antennae that have spread all over my body, the layout of my nerves. I realized I was writing a book about melancholy. It is the shield of luminous words – the most lasting of all my belongings.

If I was born somewhere in the West, this book wouldn't need to be a lyrical document, a novel with irrefutable facts – it could afford to be light reading about vampires, because objects endure in those lands, and public and private worlds are not prone to cyclical destruction as they are here. Even if one of the Western worlds is wiped out, it would be easy to replace because there are technical drawings that enable it to be rebuilt. Everything there is recorded, preserved in archives, while here we're just at the beginning of the great adventure of noting and recording, and of resuming a normal life. But we should always leave a little space for the possibility of fire and ice from heaven, or from the earth, for caution's sake. It's all too easy to misprophesy in unpredictable times. That's why I dream of a big book, in which all the people from these sad climes can be inscribed with their fears and hopes, one big book of the living that will be used for medicinal purposes. In that way, dreams and art shall become our strongest weapon.

The House of
Horrors

Mustafa Husar went out into the daylight after several hours in the hall of the Cultural Centre. He tottered over the gravel of the car park in front of the building, which slowed him down as if he was trudging through desert sand. He had been at a hypnotic seance with the fakir of the Indian Ramayana Flying Circus. The circus was actually Italian, but the troupe included several genuine hypnotists and snake trainers from India. It provided a dash of multiculturalism in a white, European company – a careful dose of spice typical of Europe, the world capital of hatred and prejudice.

He was thirsty, but he couldn't quite get his bearings and find a drinks stand to slake his thirst after that demanding, vocal stream of consciousness that had roared through the hall during his long session with the fakir. Exhausted like an actor leaving the stage after performing for several hours, Husar wandered through the L-shaped fairground that nestled up to the Cultural Centre. He couldn't easily leave now because of the throng, being hemmed in by cheerful adults and their children, flashing lights of different colours, a cacophony of screams from the merry-go-round, and models of spaceships from *Star Wars* moved by giant hydraulic rods. Their shadows flitted over his face at the speed of smoke. He recalled that he had left a beer bottle under his chair with a few swigs of lukewarm beer left inside, but that was too far to break through the circus jungle. Now he heard elephants trumpeting inside a tent, and a mass of children in the audience stood open-mouthed watching animals they'd never seen *live* before or didn't know existed – a Bengal tiger and a capuchin monkey – just as they didn't know about bananas or Milka chocolate because they'd been born during the war when such exotic foods weren't on sale.

He had lost all sense of time in the dark hall but, judging by the grey-blue sky, he concluded that dark was just beginning to fall. His head gradually cleared and he pushed aside his thoughts with the gentle movement of an imaginary hand. He needed something exciting to raise him out of his perplexity and lethargy. Without much ado, he entered the House of Horrors to give himself a good fright, so his blood would course through his veins like when the shell landed just two metres in front of him during the war. A ghostly peace reigned inside. He let his feet take him about the room of mirrors, where he was beset at every turn by distorted shapes of trolls and little demons. He kept on going, bravely, as if the lives of thousands of helpless civilians depended on his advance through the House of Horrors – he knew the expectations of those far behind the front lines perfectly well. But he wanted to free himself, to stop thinking and resolving problems that others didn't even see. He wanted to stop his redemption for collective suffering, because not even a thousand redeemers could heal people in a country where everything was defined by a war without victors. In the tunnel, with walls of a rubberized material, he was attacked by fists and merciless hands, that grabbed him by the neck, arms and legs. Ten metres from the end, where a reddish light kept blinking and going out again in the depth of the darkness, he fell to his knees. He felt as if someone was hitting him on the back of the head with a mallet and hammering him into the rubberized floor of the tunnel, but he wasn't afraid. Unexpectedly they desisted, and the mallet was gone too. He sat down on a perforated metal bench beneath a yellow light. In front of his very nose, two metres away, a yellow train rushed by at 120 kilometres per hour. He saw the rails and above them an advertisement with the face of an unnaturally beautiful woman, and on the side near the woman's ear it read: *Botox to go*. He took this to mean that Botox was a living god that walked among people.

A wind started moving through the air of that space, and he detected a familiar smell he couldn't immediately identify. He stood up from the bench and headed on wobbly legs for the poorly illuminated stairs. There was an exit with a big green Ul.

Uhlandstraße, he read on a sign and realized that this was the Berlin metro. He inhaled the fresh air on Kurfürstendamm Boulevard, where it's quite normal to have a scar on your face and you don't have to make sacrifices for the sins of the insensitive and unaware. It was early autumn and Mustafa Husar, veteran of the Army of Bosnia-Herzegovina and aspiring poet, walked through the shadows of the manicured plane trees, knowing that with every breath of Berlin air and its new, amazing smells he was forgetting all that oppressed him, all that gave him palpitations and made his heart miss a beat, as well as his arrhythmia and tachycardia. He was forgetting all the panic attacks he used to have when attempting to walk the twenty metres from his flat to the shop to buy some superfluous grocery item, just so as to check if he was able to take those twenty steps in the outside world, among people who were light years distant from him even when they brushed against his body. He was forgetting the murmur of dead planets in his ears, the twitching of the slippery creatures who encouraged him to die, and the way his arms went numb up to the elbows as he feverishly raced through town towards the emergency ward, bathed in sweat, with his brain working flat out, imagining that he was dying of a heart-attack one minute, and then thinking he was having a stroke. He forgot the very next thought and just walked straight on looking into the faces of people he was seeing for the first time, yet feeling he had known them for all eternity. He knew he would soon come across the Kaiser Wilhelm Memorial Church, which he saw for the first time in Wim Wenders's film *Wings of Desire*, then later in Matthias Koeppel's panoramic picture, and finally *for real* during a short stay in Berlin. When he came to the square where the Protestant church stood, he thought how close he was to its crippled steeple, which Allied bombers badly damaged in the Second World War, and the Germans later conserved. He marvelled at the lateral hole in the body of the church, through which a warm city breeze was blowing. He felt complete happiness and an emotional bond with chance passers-by. Then he stood for a long time and gazed at the steeple.

The elephants' bellows sobered him and he was standing firmly on his own two legs again, his feet bogged down in the coarse sharp-edged gravel of the Culture Centre's parking lot. The moments of his ordeal were over. He had had a vision that everything was at his fingertips – a new world and new smells, but it was all more than untouchable. He returned to his body. To his familiar skin and scars. The smell of dew in the grass of the town's park roused the spark of life in him. He wanted to walk the steel-blue asphalt that snails with spiral-shaped houses used to crawl out on to on rainy evenings. He melted into the crowd. Headlights from passing cars randomly lit up hidden nooks in the crowns of the trees. He heard the murmur of many voices. Others went in silence, deep in thought, with their hands behind their backs. People walked along the road, on footpaths, on tracks in the park, over grass through the darkness with the glow of cigarettes waving in their invisible hands. They made a gentle nocturnal rustle full of optimism and hope, characteristic of warm, starry nights. He melted into the crowd, infected with a sudden love for all these people. If he could, he would have embraced the whole horizon, together with the frozen celestial bodies.

The Author

FARUK ŠEHIĆ was born in 1970 in Bihać, in the Socialist Federal Republic of Yugoslavia. Until the outbreak of war in 1992, he studied veterinary medicine in Zagreb. However, the then 22-year-old voluntarily joined the army of Bosnia and Herzegovina, in which he led a unit of 130 men. After the war he studied literature and has gone on to create a body of literary work. Critics have hailed Šehić as the leader of the 'mangled generation' of writers born in 1970s Yugoslavia, and his books have achieved cult status with readers across the whole region. His collection of short stories *Under Pressure* (Pod pritiskom, 2004) was awarded the Zoro Verlag Prize. His debut novel *Quiet Flows the Una* (Knjiga o Uni, 2011) received the Meša Selimović prize for the best novel published in Serbia, Bosnia and Herzegovina, Montenegro and Croatia in 2011; and the EU Prize for Literature in 2013. His most recent book is a collection of poetry entitled *My Rivers* (Moje rijeke, Buybook, 2014). Šehić lives in Sarajevo and works as a columnist and journalist.

The Translator

WILL FIRTH was born in 1965 in Newcastle, Australia. He studied German and Slavic languages in Canberra, Zagreb and Moscow. Since 1991 he has been living in Berlin, where he works as a freelance translator of literature and the humanities. He translates from Russian, Macedonian, and all variants of Serbo-Croat. His website is www.willfirth.de.

In 2015, Firth was shortlisted for the Oxford-Weidenfeld Translation Prize and longlisted for the International Dublin Literary Award for his translation from the Serbian of Aleksandar Gatalica's *The Great War*, published by Istros Books.

istrosbooks

Istros Books is an independent publisher of contemporary literature from South East Europe, based in London, UK. We aim to show-case the very best of literature from the region to a new audience of English speakers, through quality translations.

Our 2016 titles:

DIARY OF A SHORT-SIGHTED ADOLESCENT by *Mircea Eliade*
From the perspective of a schoolboy's diary of everyday life in Bucharest in the early 20th century we are introduced to the themes of religion, self-knowledge, erotic sensibility, artistic creation and otherness, subjects that would preoccupy Eliade, one of Romania's most prominent intellectuals, until the end of his life.

BYRON AND THE BEAUTY by *Muharem Bazdulj*
Loosely based on Byron's biography, this story takes place during two weeks of October 1809, during his now famous sojourn in the Balkans. Besides being a great love story, this is also a novel about East and West, about Europe and the Balkans, about travel and friendship and cruelty.

LIFE BEGINS ON FRIDAY by *Ioana Pârvulescu*
Set during 13 days at the end of 1897, this novel follows the fortunes of Dan Crețu, alias Dan Kretzu, a present-day journalist hurled back in time by some mysterious process for just long enough to allow us a wonderful glimpse into a remote, almost forgotten world. Winner of the EU Prize for Literature 2013.

PANORAMA by *Dušan Šarotar*
Follow the narrator's extraordinary travels around Europe as he tries to reveal the inner experience of the writer in a foreign setting, far from a home that seems ever more elusive. In the manner of W. G. Sebald, this story is peppered with photographs taken by the author himself.

THREE LOVES, ONE DEATH by *Evald Flisar*
When one country is released from the oppression of a communist regime, one family decides to make the best of the new-found freedom by starting a new life in the coutryside. But freedom also comes at a cost, a fact that Flisar beautifully illustrates in this sharp, fascinating story.

NONE LIKE HER by *Jela Krečič*
A light, scintillating, witty and positive novel exploring the pains of the thirty-something generation on their quest for identity. A debut novel from one of Slovenia's leading journalists.

LOTTERY FUNDED

Supported using public funding by

ARTS COUNCIL ENGLAND